"Do you like it?" Annabelle asked

Oh, yeah.

"It's called Persuasion."

"What?"

She wiggled her tempting little red-tipped, pink-striped toes at Wagner. "My nail polish. It's called Persuasion."

"What about the stripes?"

"That's a technique one of my friends taught me. She says it never fails to grab a man's attention. She calls it 'take-me-now toes.'"

Her friend was dangerous. How easy it would be to walk to Annabelle and draw her into his arms. To learn with his fingers and lips if she wore a bra or not. To drive out the burning need to make her his.

"All work and no play makes Wag a dull boy. So before I shut the door, I plan to introduce a little play into your life."

"How do you plan to do that?"

Annabelle's fingers played with the gathered material of her skirt, lifting it an inch. "By letting you know I'm not wearing any panties."

Dear Reader,

Have you ever loved someone from afar? A man so sexy and exciting your every nerve ending sparks to life as soon as he walks into the room? You want to say something, to tell him how you feel, but every time you try, your nervous system locks down and you freeze. That's what happens to Annabelle Scott and her own mouthwatering, unattainable man.

For Annabelle, a woman who has quietly been in love with her boss for years, courage comes from the most unexpected place. Finally her true naughty nature is released, and she takes Wagner Achrom on a wild, sensual adventure he'll never forget. I hope you have as much fun reading Annabelle and Wagner's story as I did writing it.

This past year has been amazing. Right before the holidays last year, I received THE CALL that Harlequin wanted to buy *Never Naughty Enough*. Now one short year later it's in the stores. This is a dream come true for me. I've loved reading romance since my grandmother handed me my first Harlequin novel to read on the long, hot summer days.

I'd love to hear from you! E-mail me at jill@jillmonroebooks.com or visit my Web site at www.jillmonroebooks.com.

Happy reading!

Jill Monroe

JILL MONROE

NEVER NAUGHTY ENOUGH

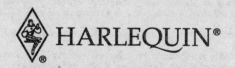

HARLEQUIN®

TORONTO • NEW YORK • LONDON
AMSTERDAM • PARIS • SYDNEY • HAMBURG
STOCKHOLM • ATHENS • TOKYO • MILAN • MADRID
PRAGUE • WARSAW • BUDAPEST • AUCKLAND

To my family and friends for all their love and infinite support.

Special thanks to Brenda Chin and Jennifer Green, who believed I could do this, and challenged me to write the best book I could.

Thanks to Kassia Krozser, Gena Showalter, Linda Rooks, Donnell Epperson, Sheila Cooper, Betty Sanders and Jenn Stone—where would I be without you? Also thanks to Angi, Tami and Beth.

I can never forget the advice and support from Merline Lovelace and Janelle Denison. The only way I can repay you is to some day pay it forward. My heartfelt thanks!

ISBN 0-373-69203-X

NEVER NAUGHTY ENOUGH

1

SHE WAS STRETCHING again.

Wagner Achrom rubbed the bridge of his nose as he watched his assistant, Annabelle Scott, slowly rotate her shoulders, first her right, then her left. Then closing her eyes, she swayed from side to side in her chair, her breasts jutting from the blue sweater she wore.

A curl of tension snaked through his body. He'd never noticed Ms. Scott's breasts before. Of course, she'd never worn a curve-hugging sweater before now. But the inviting, fuzzy material of her sweater, with the hint of flashing metallic, didn't quite fit with the cool, professional image his assistant usually projected.

Cool…at the moment Wagner was anything but cool.

He dug a finger under his collar to force a little calming air on his skin. Skin. His eyes strayed to Ms. Scott's smooth skin, flushed a pretty pink above the plunging neckline of her sweater. He'd never noticed her skin before either. But then, she never revealed anything below the top button.

Maybe they should discuss the office dress-code policy. Henceforth, sweaters were strictly forbidden.

Not that her clothes were inappropriate, just surprising since she normally wore ankle-length skirts and loose-fitting suit jackets.

His gaze was irresistibly drawn to her ice-blue sweater and his mind took another unexpected, and unwelcome, turn toward the sensual. Something easily dealt with and restrained. Well, not easily, but he *would* restrain it. He had too much at stake with the Anderson deal to let a blue sweater, and the woman wearing it, distract him.

Anderson. Oh, yeah. Right. With calm and firm determination, he reached for the file Annabelle had left on his desk. He needed to examine the latest demands before he signed, green-lighting the proposed merger between his company and theirs.

Anderson's stock would bullet up the exchange once this merger was finalized. They'd acquire free reign of his father's patents. Using the technology behind Mason Achrom's energy storage ideas, Anderson's Research and Development team planned to develop a large-scale solar-and-wind-power network, retooling and often replacing much of the aging electrical grid system. It was a far different vision than Wagner's of bringing cheap, independent power to the farms and rural areas of the world.

Anderson would gain the better end of this deal. A fact he acknowledged, but couldn't avoid grinding his teeth over. Once pegged as a corporate raider,

Wagner would have torn a small, undervalued company like Anderson apart with a few swipes of his pen, all while making a healthy profit. In the past, he'd made the best deals in the southwest. Deals where he, and the investor group he'd worked for, came out on top. But these weren't the old days, and this merger provided exactly what he desperately wanted. Cash. Cold, hard and lots of it.

With that money, he would finally put to use the only thing his dad had ever left him. To some, the lines, graphs and chemical equations resembled nothing more than scribbles. But Wagner saw what his father was never able to, those patents represented cheap, clean fuel. And cheap fuel was something others would be willing to pay millions to attain.

He hated to share the lucrative development rights to his father's patents. Except, without a capital injection, they weren't doing him any good anyway. The Anderson people could have the large-scale energy network, the short-term profitable end of the deal.

But not for long.

Wagner wasn't the type to throw it all away. He had a new project in mind. A better one. With Anderson's money, Wagner would take some of his father's unfinished ideas off the drawing board and create a small, inexpensive fuel cell. One with amazing power that could be almost instantly charged and ready to operate anything more draining than a solar calculator.

Now that his mind had successfully dulled the image of Ms. Scott's breasts, he made himself read the document word by word. A moment later, Wagner seized his red pen and underlined a key point.

A soft, feminine sigh wafted in from the outer office. Glancing up, he witnessed his always competent assistant ably reach for a manila file, while showing an amazing stretch of leg. Her softly muscled calf, her slender thigh, the—

The contract slipped from his fingers and floated to the beige carpet. As he bent to pick it up, he knocked his forehead on the metal handle of his desk. "Ow."

"Are you okay?" She'd pivoted in her swivel chair and faced him. An eyeful greeted him. Two eyefuls. Her nipp— Ms. Scott must be very, very cold. Had he turned the thermostat down? No, sweat was dribbling down his neck. The air in here was downright hot.

He shot up in his chair, rubbing his head. "Yes, fine."

"Are you sure?" Her eyebrows pulled together, as if she was concerned, and her voice sounded husky. No one had given a damn about him since his mother's death five years ago. He was oddly…what was the word? Touched.

"Fine," he told her.

She gave him a slight smile, then returned to her typing.

Wagner watched her fingers move quickly over the keyboard. Ms. Scott was the perfect assistant. Always punctual and always efficient. They'd worked together over four years now. If she'd shown concern in the past, he hadn't noticed.

Why now?

Developing an affinity was only natural. He'd been alarmed the time her car wouldn't start. When he'd checked it out for her, he'd discovered the car was so dilapidated he'd insisted she find more reliable transportation. The next day, he'd left printouts featuring several reasonably priced, dependable cars on her desk, satisfied she could handle it from there.

Yes, the concern she'd just demonstrated was born out of two people working side by side. Nothing more. And nothing like the thoughts he'd had about her moments before. *Those* thoughts had no place in their working relationship. Annabelle clicked her mouse a few times and his guilty mind shifted back to work.

Usually he liked the sound of her fingers lightly tapping the keyboard. At least it gave the office an illusion of productivity. His start-up capital long gone, he'd been dipping into his personal savings until he could count what remained without using a comma. The creditors would be swooping soon.

If this merger didn't happen, he'd be back to working for someone else. To making someone else money. To never succeed with his own vision. Wagner swallowed his distaste. He was more than a hatchet man. He aspired to build. To leave a mark.

He grabbed the file and resumed reading. He'd

driven a hard bargain to ensure autonomy for Achrom Enterprises after they moved under the new business umbrella. Although he'd sit on Anderson's board he'd still run his own shop, still be able to develop his own ideas. Anderson *would not* lawyer away those concessions from him in this final contract.

Annabelle sighed again.

The sound loosened a spiral of desire in his gut, compelling his gaze her way once more. She curved her back as she stretched, tugging her sweater taut over her breasts again. Her long, brown hair had loosened from her clip and tangled down her back, teasing the skin at her neck. And him. She looked like a woman languid from kissing.

And wanting more.

He slammed the file shut on the desk, startling her. With a darting glance his way, Ms. Scott quickly returned to her typing.

What was the matter with him? He leaned back in his chair. Ms. Scott was too valued an assistant to bear the brunt of his frustrations. Merger or sexual.

Sexual? God, yes, but when had he begun to see Ms. Scott as sexual? As far as he knew, she led as celibate a life as he did. No quiet phone calls at the office, no picture on her desk. His own desk was just as bare. And no one used his private line. Demons from the past haunted his future. Did they haunt hers, as well?

Hell, with all the sighing and key clacking, it was

no wonder he couldn't concentrate. He needed a plan and he needed it fast.

Pushing his chair back, he crossed the threshold between his office and hers.

"Ms. Scott, do you have a cramp in your back?"

She looked up with a startled expression. "Uh, no. Why?"

"With your groaning out here, I thought you were in pain."

She blinked and shook her head. Despite her sweater, leg-flashing skirt and wild, loose hair, she appeared to be the same Ms. Scott. Her desk was neat and orderly, and her coffee cup sat on a coaster.

And that's the way it would remain.

His gaze drifted from her face, but he stopped himself before he moved past her collarbone. He'd get back on track just as soon as he turned the heat up. He couldn't have her being cold.

Wagner nodded and reached for the metal door handle to his office. "Hold any calls, please. I need to concentrate on this latest counteroffer from Anderson's representative."

And, with a decisive click, he shut the door.

ANNABELLE SLUMPED in her chair and stared at the silver knob of Wagner's door. From experience, she knew she wouldn't see him for the rest of the day. He'd probably e-mail her for coffee.

She released the breath she'd sucked in when he'd reappeared, large and agitated, in the doorway, his broad shoulders practically touching the edges. A dark lock had fallen across his forehead. His hands had braced either side of the frame, his large, muscular body filling the empty space.

For one exciting minute there, she thought she'd spotted a flicker of the hunter in his blue eyes as his gaze rooted her in her chair. A tingle, starting in her belly, had spread throughout her body. Her nipples had hardened and rubbed against her sweater.

You're a femme fatale, she'd repeated in her mind.

You're an idiot, she'd corrected after he'd slammed the door. No, he hadn't slammed. Wagner would never gather enough emotion to feel the need to slam anything.

But she did.

She grabbed a pen and slammed her desk drawer shut. Then she reached for the notepad she'd hidden under the large, multiline telephone console on her desk. Wagner would never search for anything there. Not that snooping around on her desk was an activity he'd do, but sometimes he did try to make himself useful in the front office. She shuddered as she remembered the disastrous results and the paper cuts from his last attempt. She hadn't been able to find her letter opener for weeks.

Opening the pad, she clicked the pen. With long, hard strokes, she put several dark lines through her notes.

1. Wear sweater. *Banned from the closet.*

2. Sigh. *Never again.*

3. Arch your back. *Don't strain yourself.*

Her upper lip curled as she crossed through her last note. She'd printed it in all caps and had even starred the sucker. YOU'RE A FEMME FATALE.

After tossing the list aside, she removed her headset. This telephone call required holding the receiver. With quick fingers, she dialed her best friend, Katie Sloan's, number. Katie answered on the second ring.

"I give up," Annabelle told her.

"Already? It's not even ten-thirty? Did you wear the sweater?"

Annabelle glanced at Wagner's doorway and rounded her shoulders. Now she felt ridiculous in the clingy thing. "Yeah, I wore it."

"Hmm, that should have gotten some reaction."

She yanked the sweater higher on her shoulders—the plunging neckline was a little too...plunging. "This sweater's not even made from materials known in the natural world."

"Did you remember your mantra?"

You're a femme fatale.

"Yeah, I tried it. The mantra stinks." Annabelle clicked the pen again and obliterated the mantra with a few more ink swipes.

"Did you arch your back?"

"He thought I had a backache, for crying out loud. He's probably looking up the name of a good chiropractor in his Rolodex right now."

Silence greeted her from the other end of the telephone line. Annabelle suppressed a groan. Katie was rarely silent. It meant trouble. Annabelle in trouble. Since meeting in the second grade, Katie had been devising "brilliant" ideas that usually backfired with Annabelle getting the blame. In school it was detention, last year it was a weeklong rash from a sunless tanner. On her face.

"I just had a brilliant idea. It's time to bring out the big guns," Katie finally said. "Is there some way you can lock him in the supply closet with you?"

"He'd spend the whole time devising a way to buy out the door company and take over the management."

"I'm not so sure it would work. That was the old Wagner Achrom."

"True." Annabelle sat a little straighter in the chair and eyed the doorknob. That lock appeared pretty flimsy, a good safety net if she— "No, forget it. Former corporate raider or not, he'd figure a way out. Besides, I did everything but recline naked on my desk."

"Now, *that* has possibilities."

A quivering in the small of her back propelled her forward in her chair. "Out of the question." If she didn't stop this line of thought right now, Katie *would* have her convinced greeting Wagner wearing nothing but high heels and a tie, à la *Pretty Woman*, was a fabulous idea.

Annabelle pushed her glasses down lower on her nose and rubbed her eyes. "There has to be another way for him to finally notice me."

"You ever heard the phrase 'You're pumping a dry well'?" Katie asked.

"Of course I've heard it. We're in Oklahoma."

"Well, you should have paid attention to it 'cause, sister, the well's done gone dry. And I'm not sure it had much juice to begin with."

Annabelle swiveled her chair toward Wagner's door. No molding, no scrollwork. Just hard wood. Like Wagner. "Maybe you're right."

"Well, of course I'm right. Although sometimes I still think there may be something there. Remember how he was about your car?"

"He was probably only worried that his daily agenda wouldn't be typed and sitting on his desk."

"Now, girlfriend, you did that to yourself. It's one thing making a man dependent on you. It's quite another when you rig the outcome without making damn sure he knows he can't live without you."

She glanced at his closed door. "You're right. I've created a monster."

"Men." Katie didn't need to say another word. That one said it all. "Okay, I've got it," she said.

Annabelle's stomach muscles clenched in apprehension. No telling what this "brilliant" idea would involve. Probably her walking a tightrope from her desk to the copy machine in nothing but a thong and a smile.

But still, her curiosity had her wondering. "What?"

"A great new plan for this afternoon. Write this down—Nothing is more seductive than food."

"What?"

"Actually, this is brilliant. A picnic. I can see it now. The birds and bees doing their thing. His head in your lap as you feed him grapes. That's a very sexy food, by the way."

"May I remind you we're in the middle of December?" Annabelle glanced outside the large glass window lining the waiting area. "The sun may be shining right now, but how long is that going to last?"

"All right. All right. Then have it on the office floor. In fact, I like that idea better. He has that nice, long leather couch in there, too. See what we can do when we brainstorm together?"

Annabelle glanced from the black leather couches in the small waiting area to the chrome and steel of her desk and file cabinet. The office of Achrom Enterprises was designed to evoke confidence and professionalism. Not picnics. Certainly no grapes. "That would be inappropriate in the office. Besides, he's not the picnic type. For that matter, neither am I."

Katie sighed heavily. "Really, as smart as he is, I don't see why he hasn't realized you're perfect for each other. I've never met two squarer people."

"I resent that remark."

"You resemble that remark. The picnic idea will work precisely because he's not the picnic type. It will knock him completely off balance. And personally, I think throwing him for a loop is long overdue."

Katie exhaled expectedly into the phone. "Look, we can forget the whole thing if you want."

Annabelle worked the pen in her hand. "I want to give this plan a try. It's time. I'm moving on with my life. I just stamped and mailed away my last loan payment yesterday. In four weeks I'll have my degree."

She glanced around the office she'd helped Wagner create. They'd begun with such dreams and high hopes. Now he faced a merger.

Sadness and a new anticipation mixed in her heart. With her loans to cover her father's shady deals paid off and her finance degree in hand, she was finally free. Free to pursue her own dreams and goals.

"I can't stay here—I don't even want to. The only thing holding me back is him. He gave me a job when everyone else sent my résumé to the circular file, if not the shredder. He saw past my family name. He gave me a salary and responsibility, and he looks incredible in a suit."

"You got me there."

Annabelle's gaze focused on Wagner's hardwood door. "If it's not to be, then I want to close the door firmly behind me and never look back."

"Then work with me here. You don't have much time before lunch. You still have that deli on the bottom floor of your building?"

"Yes."

"Great. Then repeat after me. New mantra. You are a seductress."

WAGNER SMILED and a twist of satisfaction curled in his stomach as he red-lined a point he wanted to clarify with Anderson's front men, Smith and Dean.

Good try, fellas. Not going to work.

Did they think he would miss the clause virtually shackling him to Anderson's side for the next ten years? He might have been out of the game for the last few years, but he still knew all the tricks. Hell, he'd invented some of them.

Red slashes marked the next two paragraphs for extinction, as well. The lawyer who drew up this contract obviously didn't know Wagner's cutthroat reputation. At the age of thirty, he'd earned millions of dollars for other people. Now some four years later, some punk associate thought he could outraid him. Not going to happen.

He'd been on the inside since his mom, in blind trust, sold the family home. He'd bought his first company with the proceeds, then paid his mother back threefold from the profits of selling that company in three separate pieces. Afterwards, he didn't need to risk his own money, working instead for a top-notch investor's group. For a while, he reveled in the money. Provided the kind of things his father had never been able to give to Wagner's mother. Tasted the satisfaction of forcing out some of the very people who'd never given his father a chance.

His mother's death showed how empty and shallow Wagner's life had become. He'd made a boatload of money, but he had nothing of value. Now he'd only work for himself.

Although Wagner had stopped looking at companies as potential prey, that didn't mean his hunter instinct didn't ripple below the business suit and the trappings of small-business owner. He could spot a corporate raider sizing him up and setting a trap aimed to shaft him. Like any good huntsman, he knew how to circle around and cut the guy off before he could blink.

Forcing the smile from his face, he focused on the next page of the contract.

A knock at the door interrupted his train of thought. Ms. Scott walked in carrying a large wicker basket and a champagne bottle. He surged to his feet as she approached. "What's this?"

"We've both been working so hard and I wanted to celebrate."

His gaze shifted to the marked-up pages of the Anderson contract. Hope of an easy merger with some shreds of his former glory intact faded each time he took the cap off his pen. He didn't need a Vegas bookie telling him the odds were low on forging out everything he wanted from this contract. What he really wanted was to do the job on his own. "What's to celebrate?"

She gave him a tentative smile. "The near completion of the merger and…my degree."

Real joy for her success filled him. It was nice to see good things happen to people who deserved them. They shared a common background of dead-beat dads. He'd met Annabelle when he was at the top of his game and she was at her lowest: completely alone except for the debt her father left her. The man had stolen from his relatives and she'd vowed to repay every penny. Now with a balance sheet firmly in the black, she presumably was ready to start her life. His pleasure vanished, replaced by…apprehension? He straightened his tie and cleared his throat.

"You'll make a wonderful financial counselor," he said, dropping his pen. A touch of sadness tinged his happiness for her. She'd be leaving soon.

"I just need to finish the semester. Soon I will be helping people make better investment choices." She leaned to the side, resting the basket on her hip.

Sprinting around the desk, he reached for the handle. "Here, let me help you with that."

Her smile broadened as she handed him the basket, their hands brushing. She reached for the blanket on top of the basket, and with one motion shook it and let it fall to the ground.

"What are you doing?" he asked.

She settled herself on the faded patches of the blanket, tucking her legs beneath her, giving him a clear view down her sweater. Her cleavage was, in a word, stunning.

He had to get her out of there. He had a merger to concentrate on, not…

"Thigh or breast?" she asked.

He gulped. Chicken. She was offering him chicken. Not her delectable body. "Both."

Wagner sank to the floor beside her before he gawked further. This was her way to celebrate; she'd worked hard. If Annabelle wanted to sit cross-legged on the floor, he would let her. He owed her.

"I thought an indoor picnic would be nice. We both have to eat lunch. This way we don't have to leave the office, worry about ants, and I can still answer the telephone if needed."

Perfect sense. As always. He appreciated having Ms. Scott in the office. He'd miss her punctuality, level head and sense of order.

After pulling out two red ceramic plates from the basket, she began to lay out chicken salad and pasta. His stomach growled as the smell of warm bread hit his nose.

"Fresh from the bakery around the corner."

She spread a liberal pat of butter on her bread with efficient movements. A little of the butter landed on her finger. She brought her finger to her lips, sucking the tip into her mouth.

Their eyes met. She'd caught him staring. "Butter?" she asked.

Oh, yeah.

"Wagner, would you like butter on your bread?"

He gave himself a mental shake. "No. Better not. Thank you."

"Would you open the bottle?"

Reaching for the bottle, he tore the aluminum covering off with the ease of a man in familiar territory. In the past, he'd had many reasons to celebrate, but nothing to be proud of.

Stretching gracefully across the blanket, she placed his plate in front of his knee. Her fingers lightly grazed his leg. He felt the sensation through the wool material of his pants and he steeled his muscles not to react. Instead, he stared at her hands. He'd never noticed the fine bone structure of her delicate fingers and wrists.

Such slender hands to take on so much work. School, her job with him and he knew she did some freelance typing to lessen her considerable debt. His gaze moved upward. Such narrow shoulders to take on the burdens of her father. His eyes traveled to her mouth. Such sweet lips. Pink and full, demanding a man's kiss.

His kiss.

Something strange and unusual tightened and swelled within him and his fingers pushed harder into the softness of the cork.

With a pop, the cork flew across the room and the bubbly champagne floated down the side of the bottle. Laughing, she handed him a flute.

He smiled as he felt its weight. "Plastic?"

"Couldn't find glass."

Eating on the carpet and drinking out of plastic champagne glasses was the other side of the planet from his caviar and Cristal days. Five years ago he could clear a path to the buffet just by walking through the room. Gourmet food on the finest china had awaited him.

Somehow he liked this better.

After carefully filling the two glasses, he handed one to her. Annabelle Scott had worked with him for so long, they meshed. But he could not remember ever having a meal with her or even being so close he smelled the tantalizing vanilla scent of her shampoo or noticed the tiny dimple in her right cheek.

Except once.

He'd forgotten that one. Until now.

Two months ago, they'd worked late into the night on a project proposal. She'd fallen asleep on the couch in the corner of his office. He'd only meant to bring her a cup of coffee so she'd be awake enough to drive home. Instead, he'd found himself staring at the way her hair curled around the soft curve of her chin. The seductive roll of her hips and the tugging of her breasts against the buttons of her blouse had jerked at his body. Pure temptation.

He'd walked away congratulating himself on not making the huge mistake of kissing her awake as his instinct first had urged.

The dimple appeared in her cheek as she slowly sucked in a coil of pasta.

A spiral of desire shot through his body. Wagner looked away. The food on his plate was a much safer place to stare.

Silence settled between them. It wasn't uncomfortable, but after a few minutes, something propelled him to break it.

"How's your back?"

Her eyebrows knotted together in confusion, then she smiled. "Oh, fine. Just needed to stretch a little bit. All that studying."

A cold sweat blasted him on the back of the neck as she closed her eyes and rolled her shoulders. His gaze roamed to her breasts and he very nearly groaned. He grabbed the plastic champagne flute and downed his bubbly in one long swallow.

Then he coughed. "That's not champagne."

"No. I didn't think alcohol would be wise in the middle of a workday. That's sparkling plum cider."

"Very…interesting flavor," he said between coughing and trying to catch his breath.

"It was all they had."

Coughing a few more times, he gasped for air, not able to break the cycle. Ms. Scott reached over and patted him on the back. Her breasts swayed before his eyes. The urge to cough again assailed him. *Be an adult.* "I'm okay."

She leaned away, her eyebrows knotting again. "I have just the thing to clean your palate." She returned her attention to the basket and pulled out two large slivers of chocolate cake and a bunch of green grapes.

"The grapes aren't really in season yet, so they cost a fortune, but I just love them, don't you?"

He nearly sprang up from the blanket when her

pink tongue licked the plumpness of the grape. He imagined her tongue touching and tasting his—

What the hell was happening to him? The way she was eating made him think of nothing but sex. With Ms. Scott. Sex with Ms. Scott.

The absurdity of the idea drove him to his feet. Unfortunately he took the corner of the blanket with him. Silverware clinked off her plate and the chocolate cake flipped to the carpet. She scrambled after it.

"Ms. Scott, thank you for the lunch. I'll eat the rest at my desk. I have to go over this merger contract one more time."

Maybe he had more of the hunter left in him than he thought. His company falling about his ears, his most valued assistant about to leave him and the only thing that filled his mind was the image of her on that patchwork blanket.

Naked.

And the ideas. The first image had him laying her back on that quilt and drawing her into his arms. The second one had to do with butter, slathering and licking. He balled his hands into fists to prevent himself from acting on those ideas.

When she looked at him, her eyes were filled with something… What was it…? Hurt?

Anger, with himself and this strange, frustrating situation, made him regret his awkward, brusque behavior. "Uh, thank you, Ms. Scott. And congratulations."

With a tight nod, she scooted around on the quilt on all fours, gathering the remnants of their lunch and returning it into the wicker basket. He turned his head as her delicious backside came into view.

He was a pig.

The lid banging on the basket signaled her cleaning task was completed. "Ms. Scott."

Her eyes met his, a mixture of dread and hope evident in her gaze. "Yes?"

"I'll be working late this evening. Please lock up when you leave."

He broke out in a sweat as she shut the door behind her.

ANNABELLE SUCCESSFULLY resisted the temptation to slam the door. Instead, she stalked over to her desk, dumped the basket next to the file cabinet and grabbed the pad under the phone.

This time she retrieved a thick Sharpie marker to cross out her stupid list. She meant business.

1. Use your tongue. *Bite it the next time you feel the need to seek advice from Katie.*

2. Play with your food. *Leave that to the toddler set.*

3. Arch your back more. *Keep that up and you'll give yourself a real backache.*

The pungent odor of the marker filled the room as she colored over any trace of her latest mantra. *You're a seductress.*

Yeah. Sure. A seducer right back to work.

Pushing the paper aside, Annabelle dialed Katie's

number. She should put it on the office speed dial. Her friend answered on the first ring; she must have been expecting her call.

"Are you sticky from butter?"

"How'd you know it was me?"

"Caller ID."

"The plan tanked. I'm finished."

"Hmm."

The clicking sound over the phone line gave Annabelle a clear image of Katie in her mind. She reclined in her chair, clicking her pen between her teeth. Thinking. *Never a good sign.*

"No new plans. You're right. The well's a bust," Annabelle said. She had a plan of her own. Maybe if she agreed with Katie, her next suggestion wouldn't involve stilettos and a black feather boa.

"I don't know. I can't help but think all he needs is a nudge." Katie took a sudden intake of breath. "I've got it."

Annabelle cringed. "Maybe you shouldn't say those words again. Your last two plans backfired."

"Those plans should have worked. I'm beginning to think it's the execution. That's why I'm taking matters into my own hands. I'm overseeing the next operation."

"Katie, I'm not interested—"

"You'll start seeing another man."

Her muscles relaxed. This newest brainchild would go nowhere. "Well, first I have to choose just one from the many clamoring outside my door."

"We'll start small. There's a party tonight. Heather's roommate got married and she's throwing an 'I'm still single' bash at her apartment."

This time Annabelle's groan was audible. "No, not a party. I hate parties."

"Belle, honey, maybe it's time for you to move on. Nothing's happening there in the office. You need to search for something new. It might not be at this party, but it's a start to get your feet wet."

She cut another glance at Wagner's firmly shut door. His heart, like that door, would remain shut to her forever. She might as well get used to it. "Okay, I'll go."

"Great. See you there."

Annabelle replaced the receiver and looked back at her notebook. She ripped out her carefully prepared notes. With purposeful steps, she walked to the paper shredder, flipped the switch and rammed the pages home.

2

"WHY AM I HERE?" Annabelle shouted over the din of the crowd.

"Do you mean philosophically?" Katie teased as she slid two drinks off the makeshift bar and handed one to Annabelle.

"No, you know what I mean." Annabelle had never really fit into the singles' party scene, although this one was better than most. Someone's home always won out over a loud bar. But noise was noise. She smoothed the muscles above her eyebrows, a headache already forming. She should have worn her glasses.

Laughter drifted from the center of the room where two couples stood. Annabelle couldn't miss the uncomfortable posture and forced smile on the face of one of the women. She did not relish an evening of doing the same. She tried to hand her drink back to Katie. "This is crazy. I hate parties."

"Which is exactly why you need to be here. You need to get back into the groove. A few years ago, you were the life of the party."

"Parties are all wrong for me. See that group of guys over there. They have 'my-dot-com-start-up-went-bust-and-now-I'm-living-with-my-parents written all over them. They're scouting for a woman to bankroll their next project. Not a soul mate."

Katie raised an eyebrow. "And are you trying to find a soul mate? No, you're only trying to have a nice time, maybe have an intelligent conversation with an interesting man."

For six months, her best friend had been on a mission to give Annabelle a life—starting with the ridiculous toe ring now twisting around her index toe. Annabelle was amazed Katie still managed to gear up any energy for the project, especially after the picnic fiasco this afternoon. Of course, Katie did the easy part. Her best friend was all about suggestions.

As hard as Katie might try to zap her into some semblance of hipness, Annabelle could never match Katie's innate coolness from her pink gel-spiked hair to her glimmer eye shadow. Glimmer. She'd just gotten used to glitter. And this party was a mistake.

Yes, it was time to leave. "Do you see any coasters?" Annabelle asked.

Katie shrugged, lifting her tank top higher and emphasizing her belly ring. "Just set it anywhere."

Annabelle shook her head and scanned the room. Some deep-rooted sensibility prevented her from putting a glass on bare wood.

Katie straightened her back and smiled. "Hey, Jeff's over there. Let's join him."

Annabelle glanced over to where Katie was pointing, then quietly groaned. She should have guessed. The group consisted of all men. Parties where her best friend felt an obligation to throw her into every cluster of eligible men were especially tiring. "Oh, not those guys."

"What's wrong with them?"

Too many reasons. They didn't have blue eyes. They didn't have a scar above their right eye or make every atom in her body jump.

They weren't Wagner.

Annabelle shook her head. "I just can't believe I left the office early for this."

A line formed between Katie's eyebrows. "I'll have you know, leaving at five-thirty is not early for most people. Especially on a Thursday night."

"What's the big deal about Thursday?"

Katie rolled her eyes. "Pre-weekend party. You'd think you'd never been to college at all."

"I still have to go in early tomorrow. We're working on a big project." She searched for a coaster to set her drink. "In fact, I had a hard day at the office and I need to get some sleep. Thanks for inviting me, but I'm going to head on home."

"Mr. Monochrome working you all hours of the day and night?" Katie stomped her foot, sending her ankle bracelet jangling. "How is everything in the—sheesh, what is it he does?"

"Solar cells. And it's going extremely well. By replacing the silicone conductors currently used in the photovoltaic—"

Katie held up a hand. "Wait, sorry. Forget I asked. I'm not up to a conversation like the 'how batteries really work' discussion we had last week. I wasn't able to get nickel-metal hydride out of my head for several days."

Annabelle stood taller, ready to defend Wagner. "It won't be long before his ideas revolutionize the way we power up our laptops and heat our homes. Besides, stop calling him Mr. Monochrome. That look happens to be very stylish and there's a lot to be said about understatement."

"Yes, but he wore it before that millionaire show made it popular. And that trend's long gone."

Annabelle turned toward the door, drink in hand. "I'm leaving. What kind of place doesn't have coasters?"

Katie waved her hand. "Forget I said anything about Mr. Color Deficient. You need to think of someone other than him and this party is the place to do it."

"We've been through this before."

"I know and I'll shut up. I just want you to stop wasting your time on him and think about meeting someone new. You've been working for him, what, four years? Honey, I know it's hard to hear and it's hard for me to say, but the guy is never going to notice you. He's too involved in his company and proving that he's not his father."

Annabelle shook her head. "It is *not* hard for you to say that, because you say it all the time. I'm no longer interested in Wagner Achrom. I'm giving him up, but I'm staying because he pays well. Very well. Don't forget he gave me a job when I had more bills than prospects. I owe him a lot. So stop giving me lectures."

"Uh-huh, right." Katie nodded toward the throng of men again. "Tell you what, we'll go over there and you say just one sentence and then we'll leave. No more hard time."

Katie might be just this side of wild, but she also had an enticing smile. The kind that could convince Annabelle that clandestinely taping an Out of Order sign on the baseball coach's hat was a good idea, or the kind that cheered her up after Hailey Griffin stole the heart of the cute guy in geometry.

Annabelle lifted an eyebrow. "Promise?"

"Promise. But your sentence can't be 'goodbye.' Besides, we're here to have a good time. And to celebrate you finally getting your pigskin."

"That's lambskin."

"We'll worry about that later." With a wink and a flick of her red hair, pink highlights flashing, Katie looped her arm through Annabelle's and sashayed through the various clusters of people all trying to have a good time.

"Hi, Katie, who's your friend?"

That was about as subtle as a high-school sophomore. Annabelle tried to hide her cringe. He obviously didn't remember, but she'd met Jeff before. His clothes reminded her of the Web sites he designed. All flash, no substance. Katie should know by now she'd never be attracted to that type of guy.

"Hi, Jeff, this is Annabelle." Katie gave her a delicate push and she nearly stumbled into his shoulder.

He caught her, his hand lingering on her elbow. "Hiya, Annie. What do you do?"

Get irritated when people call me Annie. This guy would wear his ballcap backward. She just knew it. And what happened to the guys who just talked to a woman's boobs? Jeff checked her out all right, but in a way that suggested he was mentally calculating the cost of her shoes, clothes and jewelry. Annabelle cleared her throat. "I'm an administrative assistant."

His five-hundred-watt smile dimmed. An assistant probably didn't fit into his success plan. "Nice to meet you. Mike here was just telling us he's learning hypnosis."

Annabelle couldn't help it—she laughed.

Mike straightened and turned to her. Now, this one *did* wear his ballcap backward. A sure sign he hadn't grown up and left his college days behind. "You don't believe in hypnosis?"

"Nope." There. She'd said something. Now they could leave.

Katie shook her head. "No subject, no predicate, no leaving," she whispered.

Unfortunately, from the expectant faces surrounding her, they also expected more conversation.

"You really don't believe in hypnosis?" Jeff asked.

"Well, I accept the power of suggestion, but as far as going under and changing your personality, I don't think that could happen."

Memories of her father's ugly cons suddenly crushed that last bit of hope that she might actually have a nice time at this party. Her father had been a pro with the hypnosis scam. He'd promised them a cure through hypnosis. Smoking, overeating, nail-biting, whatever. While there were plenty of well-meaning trained professionals in the world who could aid someone with strategic hypnotic suggestion, her father was neither trained nor well-meaning. With his charm and charisma people readily opened their checkbooks. She tamped down the familiar surge of guilt she felt every time she remembered one of her father's scams.

Jeff laughed. "Great. Then you won't mind being a volunteer. Mike was just looking for a victim."

Annabelle whipped her head toward Jeff. "What?"

"I can't back away from that kind of challenge," Mike said.

Annabelle reached for a lock of hair and twisted it around her finger. Twisting—a return of a bad habit. Normally, she wore her hair up in a tidy and simple bun, but Katie had insisted Annabelle's brown locks had to "cascade" down her back. She hated how unruly her curls must appear.

"You ready?" Mike asked, draping an arm around her shoulders.

Her hair issues appeared not to daunt Mike; he

had a point to make. After spouting off, she couldn't very well say no now. It would be fun to prove them wrong. Besides, what could letting him *try* to put her under hurt? It wouldn't work and Katie would owe her. Big time. Crossing her arms over her chest, she sighed. "Lead the way."

She'd learned all the cons, scams and sleights of hand at the knee of a pro—her dad. Mike's brand of backroom hypnosis didn't stand a chance.

Mike laughed, then cupped his hands around his mouth. "Hey, Heather, can we use your old roommate's room?"

Annabelle winced as all eyes in the room turned her way.

"No one's in the back bedroom. We can have a little privacy there," Mike told her.

Heather raised one arched eyebrow. "What are you going to do back there?"

"Nothing wicked," he assured. "A challenge. Annabelle here doesn't think I can put her under hypnosis."

"Sounds like fun, and seeing Annabelle put under…this I've got to see. Come on, Kelli. I can show you the bedroom while we're in there and you can see if you think it will be big enough for your drafting board."

Good to know Heather could multitask—throw a coasterless party with ease, aid and abet a delusional male in the name of fun, all while brokering her next potential roommate.

Jeff led the growing group down the narrow hallway. He opened the door and they all filed into the nearly empty bedroom. Only a desk, lamp, chair and bare mattress, angled against the wall, remained.

"Shelley's going to pick up her desk and lamp tomorrow, but the mattress you can use since she and her fiancé are getting a queen-size bed," Heather announced.

"Ladies, please. We need to create an ambience."

Heather laughed. "Whatever. I used to date you, Mike—I know all about your, uh, ambiences."

Mike closed the door behind the last person, positioned the desk chair in the middle of the room and gestured to Annabelle that she should sit down, which she did. He flipped on the beat-up banker's lamp. "Hey, someone switch off the overhead lights."

One of the women giggled when darkness flooded the room. "Why do I feel like we're in for a session of light as a feather, stiff as a board?" Katie whispered.

"Oh, hey, I remember that game."

Memories of late nights, bowls of M&M's and bras in the freezer filled Annabelle's memory. "That game we used to play at slumber parties? We could never get it to work on me. Just don't let anyone put my hand in a bowl of warm water."

Katie laughed.

Mike cleared his throat. "It'll need to be quiet to pull this off. Okay, Annabelle, you're getting very sleepy."

She chuckled. "Oh, please. Can you come up with a line a little more original than that?"

Mike rolled his sleeves up to his elbows. "Just work with me. Close your eyes and clear your mind. Forget about everyone in the room."

She exhaled sharply, but closed her eyes. The sooner he tried to hypnotize her and failed, the sooner she could go home and sink into a warm mountain of bubbles in her bathtub.

"Go back in your memory. Search it for a time when you were at your most relaxed."

She opened one eye. "I'm never relaxed."

"It's true. I've never seen her relaxed," Katie said.

"Okay, then a favorite memory." Mike made a hand motion to indicate she needed to close both her eyes.

Favorite memory? Now, that was easy. That would have to be the time when she'd worked late with Wagner and fallen asleep on the soft leather couch in his office. He'd woken her up with the smell of fresh coffee under her nose. She'd opened her eyes and nearly fell into his deep blue ones, so much more alluring without his glasses. His eyes had darted to her mouth.

For one heart-stopping moment, she'd thought he might kiss her.

"Have you got one?" Mike asked, his voice slowly swimming toward her.

It took her a moment to answer. "Yes." Her voice sounded heavy and slurred. Why was she having so much trouble saying only one word?

"Good. Now keep thinking of that time. Concentrate on the good feelings that memory brings to you.

Let everything else fall into the background but those feelings and my voice."

"Yes. Background. Coffee," Annabelle repeated. She swayed a bit in her chair. Through the fog of memory, she felt a hand on her shoulder, steadying her.

"Maybe you should stop, Mike."

Was that Katie's voice? Weird. She sounded upset. What was she doing in Wagner's office? The voice faded. Annabelle must have made a mistake. The scent of Wagner's cologne filled her senses and she felt the delicious sensation of anticipation as his lips almost touched hers. She arched forward, closer to—

"What should we do?" Heather whispered.

"We should give her a suggestion. What does she need? Does she have any bad habits?" Mike asked.

Annabelle fought through a haze of vaporous words and ever-dimming darkness. Who was talking? No one was in the office with them. It must be a client outside the door. Back to Wagner...

"What she needs is to forget about work once in a while. Take a day off."

"Great. You'll be spontaneous." The words, spoken next to her ear, made no sense. She squeezed her shut eyes tighter. Annabelle didn't want talking, she wanted to return to her beautiful memory. Couch. The smell of coffee.

"You'll crave marshmallows." Marshmallows for coffee? Annabelle thought Kelli, Heather's possible roommate, sure had some weird ideas.

"You'll be a sex fiend," someone blurted.

Katie gasped. "Oh, Jeff. Take that one back."

"What's the difference? This isn't working anyway."

"Yes, it is. Look at her." Was that Mike?

"Just change it," Katie told him, her voice growing more and more concerned.

What a weird dream.

"Okay, you'll be daring, sexually."

"Let's give her something she could really use. I know, you'll enjoy doing sit-ups," Heather said.

"Your thighs won't bother you," Kelli said, her tone wishful.

"You'll run naked through Bricktown Ballpark."

Mike cleared his throat, cutting off any objection. "Okay, Annabelle, when I turn on the light, you won't remember any of this, but the suggestions will remain with you."

"Oh, come on, Mike. Not fair." There was Katie's voice again.

"Okay, okay. I was only joking. I'll take the suggestions away and leave her only with a nice, rested feeling."

Light flooded the room. A shock of awareness scorched through her body and she struggled to open her eyes.

A young woman stood in the open doorway, her hand on the light switch. "Oops, sorry, didn't know you all were in here. What's going on anyway? A séance?"

"Oh, no," someone said.

Who was in the room with her? And Wagner? Wait a minute, she wasn't on a couch. She was sitting in a chair. The scent of Wagner's coffee had disappeared.

Annabelle blinked a few times as her eyes adjusted to the bright light. Six faces turned toward her expressing varying shades of alarm. If she hadn't been self-conscious before, she definitely was now. "Why are you all staring at me like that?"

Katie cleared her throat. "Belle, are you okay?"

Annabelle shrugged. "Sure, fine."

"What about the…" Her friend's voice trailed off as she shot a pointed look in Mike's direction.

With a few odd glances at one another, the rest of the group dispersed quickly from the room. Actually, they almost looked as if they were making a break for it. Mike had lost the carefree expression he'd worn earlier. His eyebrows were raised and his shoulders tense. He appeared borderline anxious.

"Annabelle, don't you remember?" Tight lines strained Katie's face. She looked worried. *Strange.* Annabelle felt great—there was nothing wrong with her.

You're getting sleepy. Now she remembered why they were all in this room and why everyone was acting so odd. Annabelle suppressed a giggle.

"Oh, the hypnosis thing? Sorry, Mike, it didn't seem to do anything. Look, I'm a little tired, though, and I'd just like to go home now."

"You're sleepy? Great. For a minute there I

thought you'd be stuck with all those crazy…never mind." Mike smiled and quickly exited the room.

Katie sighed what sounded like a breath full of relief. "Whew."

"Never knew you all would be so thrilled at me being tired," Annabelle said as she stood and stretched.

Her dearest friend smiled. "It's nothing. Thanks for coming out with me tonight. I know it's not your thing. But, Annabelle, please think about what I said earlier."

"About what?"

"About your boss. You can't move on, unless you, well, move on. Go home and get some sleep."

"Oh, I'm not tired. I actually feel really rested. I was just saying that to get rid of Mike and all his weird hypnosis stuff."

The color behind Katie's glimmer makeup faded. She opened and closed her mouth, tapping her foot. "Oh no."

Annabelle stopped stretching her back at the flicker of worry. This wasn't good. Come to think of it, most everyone had hightailed it out of the bedroom with varying degrees of worry and anxiety etched on their faces.

Why was everyone acting so weird? And Katie led the pack in the odd behavior.

"What's the big deal?" Annabelle asked.

Her friend tugged at the lining of her sleeve. "You

were supposed to wake up refreshed and you said you were tired and—"

Annabelle shook her head and made a beeline for the door. "Katie, what are you talking about? I couldn't have been in the chair for more than a few minutes." She clinked the ice in her glass. "See? I still have my drink."

"A few minutes? Annabelle, you sat in that chair for at least fifteen. Maybe we should find Mike again and have him—"

"Relax. I'm fine. Maybe with all the dark lighting I dozed off for a bit. You know how I could always take catnaps in school. Come to think of it, I did have a nice minidream. Maybe that's why I'm feeling recharged. Besides, I'm immune to hypnosis, believe me." She grabbed her purse and dropped her glass onto the oak end table.

"What, no coaster?" Katie asked, a line creasing between her eyebrows.

Annabelle lifted a shoulder. "Who needs 'em?" And she made a hasty escape out the door, but not before hearing Katie's gasped intake of breath.

AFTER QUICKLY WEAVING through the mishmash of parked cars, Annabelle unlocked her used, but reliable, Volvo, fired up the engine and took off. At least Katie didn't try to follow her. What was the big deal? So she didn't use a coaster…that didn't mean she'd been hypnotized.

She'd seen her share of hypnosis scams. Her father's "clients" had sought him out to break bad habits, but the main thing he'd managed to make disappear was their money. Heck, she could write a textbook on the beaut her father had operated in Kansas. That time he'd offered a free session and people from the simply curious to the truly desperate flocked to the storefront he'd decked out to look as professional as any dentist's office.

Of course, getting them through the front door was his sole goal. Once inside, he'd introduce them to his special vitamins, drinks and eventually the "investment club" only for his best clients. Hypnosis was only the hook—it was her father's charisma and the sheer force of his personality which really mesmerized his unsuspecting patrons.

It was amazing how her father had become so proficient in "relieving" so many people of their money but never managed to keep any of it. When he'd died, he'd left her a mountain of bills, mostly money owed to her relatives. She'd never forget the hours after her father's funeral when her aunt and uncle had asked about the savings and stocks her father had "invested" for them. And the sickening feeling of telling them they'd been fleeced. Like so many others in her father's wake.

But this time had been different. This time he'd hurt family. A few weeks shy of her eighteenth birthday, she'd taken her GED and went to work to support her aging aunt and uncle. She'd also shed any remnants of the carefree teenager she'd been.

A self too much like her father.

Annabelle turned off the radio, letting the road noise be her music. What she'd told her friend was true. The tired excuse was just that, an excuse. She was more than fine, she felt exhilarated, charged with energy.

Nor was she ready to go home. She loved driving through Oklahoma City at night. A leisurely car ride around the lake would buoy her lifting spirits higher. Although she wouldn't admit it to Katie, that party was exactly what she'd needed, after all. With a few deft turns of the steering wheel, she easily navigated the suburban streets and headed north toward Lake Hefner.

Some of her favorite memories were set around this lake. Several times while she had been in school, her father had signed her out and driven her to this very area. They'd sat on the hard rocks outlining the lake and fed the ducks bread. He'd said they were playing hooky together. She'd loved those special times. Now she recognized it as one more sign of her father's gross irresponsibility.

She rolled down the windows to let the night air chase away the blues. Thoughts of her father always made her feel blue. The dark water lapped against the rocks, awakening her senses. Tonight turned out to be one of those singular, beautiful December evenings, warm with just a hint of a breeze.

The night air caressed her skin. It was a reminder that the promising days of spring would welcome her, if she could just get through the winter.

But right now, her life didn't hold much hope.

Maybe Katie was right. Maybe it was time to fire up the old résumé. Wagner knew of her eventual goal to work as a financial counselor. She looked forward to helping people bail themselves out of debt and learn better spending habits. Leaving Wagner was only a matter of time. What she told Katie this afternoon was true. She was ready to move on.

Maybe it was time to stop fantasizing about her boss. Yeah, right. When, in the past four years, had she not gone to bed dreaming of Wagner Achrom?

Originally, the plan had been to serve as his administrative assistant until she completed the final credits of her degree and paid her father's debts.

When her feelings had changed she wasn't sure. Wagner was unlike any man she'd ever known. A powerful, respected and maybe even feared businessman, he'd walked away from a successful career as a corporate raider to set up his own company. Smart and shrewd, not a man who could be taken in by someone like her father. And whenever he looked at her with those dark blue eyes of his, she very nearly melted onto her swivel chair. Magnetic, confident and gorgeous, Wagner was a man who could appreciate order and precision. How could she not have fallen in love with him?

Annabelle pounded her palm against the steering wheel. Why did she have to be such an idiot? Wagner only had two things on his mind—building his

business and keeping it at the top. And she didn't figure into either one of those goals.

What she needed was to forget about work once
in a while. Take a day off.

Katie had been telling her to do that for years, but
until this moment, it never sounded like a good idea.

That settled things. She would start the weekend
early. She was taking Friday off. Hey, she was due.

Flipping on her signal light, she turned right into
a grocery-store parking lot. She hadn't planned on
shopping this evening. In fact, she'd never been in this
store, didn't know the layout. Usually, she hated not
having an idea of where the items she needed were,
walking the aisle clueless. But then, she didn't know
what she needed tonight. She just craved…some-
thing. Something sweet and full of calories. Yeah, that
was precisely what she needed. Yummy.

WAGNER ACHROM LIKED nothing more than an early
Monday morning. He despised the society-imposed
restrictions on working weekends. How was a man
supposed to build a business that way?

He flipped on his office light, powered up his computer and then scanned his desk.

And scanned it again.

Something wasn't right. His desk was…bare.
Where was his day calendar? No coffee cup was
waiting for him on the coaster, either. Annabelle always left those two essential items on his desk before
he arrived. How was a man supposed to start his

day without knowing what he needed to do and without the essential caffeine jump-start?

Wagner stalked back into the outer office. She wasn't there. In fact, there was no sign she'd even come in this morning. The blinds remained closed and her headset was still looped over the telephone. This didn't bode well for a productive Monday. Especially after she hadn't come to work on Friday.

Maybe he should call Ms. Scott. With a wary downward glance, he eyed the multiline telephone on her desk. He hated that phone. His cell would work quite nicely. But before he could press the speed dial for her number, he flicked the cell case closed. Ms. Scott would be here. She'd promised on Friday. And his assistant always kept her promises.

Feeling at a loss, he returned to his office and reclined in the executive chair, which never failed to ease his lower-back muscles. Annabelle had picked it out, always anticipating what he needed. He peered into the outer office, willing her to be there.

No reason to let this little setback throw off his day. So she was late. Everyone could be late once in a while. Once. *Once* being the key word.

He had to keep his wits about him to seal the Anderson merger. That merger remained crucial for the realization of his own ideas. All he'd worked toward over the last four years, the promise he'd made to his mother, to himself, that he'd leave his cutthroat job and find a use for his dad's patents centered on this deal's success. It would work because he'd make it.

He drummed his fingers on his desk. This was crazy. He'd built his business from the ground up. From nothing. His entire operation didn't come to a standstill simply because he didn't have a piece of paper waiting for him on his desk.

But first he needed coffee. He didn't have time to run to the coffee shop as he had on Friday. With purpose, he strode to the breakroom. They called it a room, but it was little more than a storage closet with a table, two chairs, a minifridge and coffeemaker. A coffeemaker, which he had no idea how to operate.

First things first. A paper filter. He searched all over the small space, but couldn't find a single one. In desperation, he opened the coffee bin, hoping Annabelle might have left a clean filter in there as she tidied up the area before leaving last week. He yanked on the bin handle. When had they gone to this funny little cone thing instead of good, sturdy paper filters?

Wagner spooned in what looked like enough grounds, pushed the bin home and flipped the switch. He watched as the coffee dripped into the carafe.

The dark aroma drifted to his nose and he relaxed in satisfaction. It smelled like coffee should. Why was he worried? He'd made coffee plenty of times.

A few times.

At least once.

The front door opened and closed. Annabelle

must have arrived. Good. Now maybe he could get some work done. He grabbed two mugs and poured the coffee. He'd never made Annabelle coffee before. But it seemed like the thing to do. He'd taken two steps when he stopped.

What was that sound?

Was that humming he heard from the front office? Was Annabelle humming? Annabelle never hummed. It was sort of—what was the word?— sweet. He kind of liked the sound of it.

She was obviously in a good mood, obviously feeling better. He'd been concerned when she'd taken a personal day on Friday. Wagner leaned one shoulder against the wall. He'd never really noticed Annabelle ever having a mood. That was one of the reasons that they worked so well together. And she'd been working her tail off these last few weeks. After this merger, he could hire more staff to ease her load. Hopefully he'd never be this low on employees again.

He watched as she leisurely removed her pink lightweight jacket and draped it over the back of her chair. He'd never figured her for a pink kind of woman. Nor as someone who draped clothing on the back of a chair. But she did good things for pink— it was a perfect foil for the warm brown of her eyes.

What was he thinking? And about Ms. Scott. Wagner shook his head to loosen the hold of his bizarre thoughts. She'd probably be horrified if she knew the directions his mind had been taking lately. Mostly south.

He watched in fascination as she pulled a tiny ivy plant from a plastic grocery bag and placed it on her desk. As she leaned forward, a lock of her long, brown hair fell across her face. "You have curly hair," he said.

Annabelle glanced up, a curl falling over her left eye. Her pink lips curved into a welcoming smile. He hadn't noticed how sweet her lips looked before, either.

"What?" she asked, her eyebrows drawn in confusion.

He pointed with his coffee cup. "Your hair. I've never noticed how curly your hair is."

Annabelle smiled briefly and smoothed the curls behind her ears. "The curl's natural. I never really liked it much, but this morning for some reason, I felt like wearing my hair down."

Before he could utter another inane, obvious comment, Wagner placed one of the mugs on her desk. "I didn't see you at your desk when I came in. I can't remember the last time you were late."

That strange, swelling sensation filled him again as he watched her roll out her desk chair and sit down. After a few more moments of fiddling with things on her desk, she turned to look at him. Her face scrunched when her eyes left his face and lowered to his clothes. "I've never been late."

Scratching his temple, he did a mental overview. "Come to think of it, you haven't."

She didn't say anything. In fact, Annabelle just sat

staring at his tie. He glanced down. Nothing on the black silk. He flicked a piece of lint off his matching black shirt.

"I need you to fax a few things from the Marsh file and please pull my calendar." He turned to leave.

"Nah."

He stopped halfway to his office door and turned around. "Excuse me?"

"I don't think so."

"What?" he asked.

"You know, you could use a little color."

"What?" he asked again, feeling like an idiot.

"In your wardrobe, a little red or maybe something blue to match your eyes."

"Annabelle, are you sick? I can't afford to have you sick right now, not with this big merger deal and the solar-cell tests."

"No, in fact I feel great. Best night's sleep I've had in a long time. I feel really rested."

"Good." He pointed to her computer. She still hadn't powered it on. That's where she kept his master calendar file. "Are you going to get the Marsh file?"

"I already told you no. I really don't feel like working today."

Wagner fought down his confusion. Annabelle had said no, but she'd said it with a smile that made him think boycotting work today was about as impressive as the invention of the fax machine. He was almost about to agree with her.

Merger. Work. Coffee.

"Annabelle, I insist you go to the doctor. Leave. Right now. In fact, don't come back until you have some kind of doctor's note."

An odd expression entered her eyes as she stood. A look he'd never seen before in those serious and decisive brown depths. Annabelle grabbed him by the tie and pulled him toward her. Caught unaware, he braced his hands on the smooth top of her desk.

Her breath warmed his cheek. She planted her lips firmly on his and kissed him.

For a moment he was too shocked to move. But then his brain registered the softness of her lips, the downright sexiness of her perfume, the hint of her breasts touching his chest. The taste of something sweet on her lips. Long-forgotten desire shot through his body as she released him.

Gripping her shoulders loosely, he pulled her close. She smiled as his lips neared hers. "I quit."

3

"WHAT?"

Wagner wore such a delightful expression of confusion, she almost felt like kissing him again. Almost. Belle was having too much fun at his bewilderment to let him off the hook.

Belle.

Before her father's arrest, people had called her Belle. Katie still did; she liked it. Right now she felt like a Belle. Lighthearted and fun—the way she used to be.

Belle had never seen Wagner the slightest bit perplexed. He epitomized control. Now he looked downright puzzled.

How delightful.

Man, he was something else. She'd worked for him for years and yet whenever he flashed those indigo eyes of his in her direction, her toes still curled. And his mouth…

She still felt the impression of his lips, strong and perfect, against hers. The controlled strength of him beneath her fingertips. He lived up to the fantasy. She'd wanted to kiss him for four years.

She watched as his lips moved. Forming words. *Oh, great, he'd been talking.* She cleared her throat. "Were you saying something?"

"Are you having trouble concentrating, too? This is serious."

She waved her hand. "No, no, no. I'm fine. Do you want me to finish out the rest of the day or go ahead and pack up now?"

An odd expression crossed his face, as if for a moment he was contemplating a world without her and didn't like it. A small surge of hope formed in her heart, then died. This was Wagner Achrom. More likely he was envisioning an *office* without her in it. Judging from this morning's behavior, he didn't do well around the office without her.

Good. Time he knew it.

The muscles of his face relaxed and returned to his normal neutral expression. He stole a quick look down at his watch. "You're not serious about quitting. You're delirious."

"Well, it certainly wasn't because I was bowled over by that kiss." That would teach him to look at his watch around her. She forced a light yawn. "In fact, I could go for a good nap right now."

His blue eyes narrowed. "Are you saying there's something wrong with the way I kiss?" He almost growled the question.

"Well, you have to admit, it *was* a little stiff."

Wagner knotted his tie a little tighter. Funny, she'd never noticed that little nervous habit of his. But now that she thought about it, he *did* become stiff, more so than usual, when uncomfortable.

She watched as he swallowed. "Stiff?" he demanded.

"Oh, yes, very. Maybe you should come over here and try again."

Wagner cleared his throat and glanced toward the door. "We're moving into an area that's very uncomfortable to me. There are issues of sexual impropriety and the law—"

"Oh, please." She gestured toward him. "Like some judge wouldn't take one look at your tie and know there's nothing going on in this office but business."

"Get your purse or whatever it is you need. Doctor time. In fact, I'm taking you to mine. Let's go." His fingers were firm yet gentle at her elbow.

Annabelle shook her head. "Oh, Wag, I'm not going to a doctor. I feel great. The best I've felt since…well, I'm not sure when."

She felt great when she pulled him to her. He felt great beside her.

Shaking his hand off her elbow, she returned to her chair. "I have work to do. I've decided to stay, at least until the Anderson merger is complete. Don't you have something for me to fax?" she reminded him.

Wagner didn't budge. "Get your purse, Annabelle. Now, or I will throw you over my shoulder and carry you."

She waved him away. "Go back into your office. Shoo. Shoo."

Wagner Achrom wasn't a man people usually shooed. Workaholic. Ruthless businessman. Dangerous in the boardroom. Amazing entrepreneur. These were all terms normally used to describe him. He obviously didn't know how to approach this new situation. But she knew what he *would* do. Go back into his office, analyze this new development from every angle and come up with a plan of attack.

As if on cue, he turned and headed for his office, the usual controlled urgency of his walk gone. She could have sworn she saw Wag fidget with his tie again. Wag. She liked this new nickname for him. She'd discovered something about Wag. He didn't like being told his kiss had left a little to be desired. And she discovered a little something about herself, too. She liked making Wagner Achrom uncomfortable.

ANNABELLE MANAGED to pick up the telephone on the fourth ring. "Achrom Enterprises."

Katie laughed. "For a minute there I didn't think anyone was going to answer the telephone. It rang several times."

"Well, my days of dashing to answer the telephone are over. Actually, it was really stupid anyway. What's the difference in answering on the first ring or the fifth?"

"I'm sorry, I thought I was talking to Annabelle Scott. Is she there?"

Annabelle leaned back in her chair and propped her legs on the desk. "Ha-ha. Actually, you won't be talking to me much longer at this number. I told Wag I quit this morning."

"What? Why?"

"After I took Friday off, I—"

Katie's groan interrupted her. "This is sounding bad."

"No, it was great. I needed to forget about work once in a while. Take a day off."

"That's just what I said on Thursday."

"Really? I don't remember that. When?"

Another low, pained groan was her answer.

"Katie, are you okay?"

"I'm trying to decide. Tell me, how did Mr. Decolor take the news of your resignation?" Katie asked, her tone slow and measured.

"You're slipping. That's not nearly as creative as Mr. Monochrome."

"I'm under stress. Work with me. What did Mr. Achrom do?"

"He insisted I go to the doctor, but I just shooed Wag into his office."

"You shooed him? Half the people in this city are afraid to be anywhere near the man. And where did this Wag come from?"

Annabelle looked at his office door. Although he'd opened the door and stalked her with his gaze a few times, after pointedly delivering the Marsh file, the heavy maple door remained firmly closed. Just like the man.

Or was it?

Before he'd shut the door, oh, so resolutely, he'd stopped by her desk several times. Other than the uncharacteristic file delivery, those instances she might possibly call false pretenses. If she didn't know the man better. Wagner wasn't a man who needed made-up excuses. He just did what he wanted.

Maybe what he needed was a few changes. She'd bet her accumulated comp time his boxers were the same color as his suit. As his shirt. As his tie. As his shoelaces. Change was good. Wag.

"I'm calling him Wag now. Don't you like it? Kinda softens him up, don't you think?"

"No, I don't think. There is nothing soft about the man. Belle, let's meet for lunch. There's something I want to talk to you about. It's important."

"Oh, I can't. I'm getting my nails done on my lunch break."

Katie took a deep, slow breath. "You scheduled a manicure?"

"Sure. I thought you'd be happy. You're always after me about my 'short sensible nails.' I was thinking something along the lines of vixen red."

Katie mumbled something under her breath that sounded like "This is really serious" and sighed. "Then wait there for me after you get off work. Actually, maybe you should pack up and go home now before you do any more damage. Think about avoiding Wag, uh, Wagner, altogether. Tomorrow maybe I can explain—"

Something tight and unwanted unfurled in her

chest. Suddenly, she didn't want to talk to Katie anymore, didn't want to hear what her best friend had to say. "I gotta go now. Wag left me a million things to do."

"I thought you quit."

"Well, after the kiss, I gave my decision a little more thought. He definitely needs another shot."

"Kiss? What kiss?"

"Bye, see you after work."

"Wait—"

Annabelle replaced the receiver, then flicked the headset into her top desk drawer. That efficient little device had become a drag. Why in the world had she thought it made sense? Her desk appeared much nicer now. Hmm. It was almost eleven. She should probably do a little work. Faxing.

As she reached for the Marsh file Wagner had left on her desk, an intense curiosity caused her hands to tingle. Marsh…something about that—

In seconds, she faced her computer, her fingers quickly typing her request into the Internet search engine.

Sometime later, Wag burst from his office and marched to her desk. "Annabelle, I had a ten-thirty conference call with Smith and Dean. Dean just e-mailed me wanting to know what the hell happened."

"Did you forget? I printed out your calendar. It should be in the tray."

"You always leave it on my desk. It's there when I arrive. This isn't like you at all."

Hmm. Clearly, she'd been making things too easy for him. "I've been very busy."

"Did you get those items faxed?"

"Nope, but I did have a very productive morning."

A look of almost comical relief crossed his face. "Good."

She pointed to the screen. "Yes, I spent a lot of time on the Internet exploring the various sites about marshmallows. Something has been swirling in the back of my mind and when I saw that Marsh file, it all clicked. I even bought some Thursday night. I couldn't put my finger on why, but now I know. They're just plain delicious. And you wouldn't believe the fascinating stuff about them. In fact..." Belle opened her bottom desk drawer and bent down. Where was that package?

Wagner cleared his throat. "I've decided to try this morning again."

Glancing up, she met his gaze. Ah, he wore that serious expression again. She could change that with a single question. "The kissing part?"

He straightened his tie. "No, not the kissing part. Are you trying to be difficult on purpose?"

Did she see a flush? Good. She returned to her search.

"Annabelle. Stop rummaging in your desk and pay attention. What is with you today? And what are you looking for anyway?"

She produced a bag and plopped it on the middle

of her desk. "These. You wouldn't believe the selection at the store. Marshmallows covered in sugar, marshmallows covered in chocolate. Then I saw these. Aren't they cute? So small and all different colors. Do you want one?"

"No, I do not want one. I want my calendar on my desk, my faxes faxed and the old Annabelle Scott back."

"All you have to do is ask."

Wag's face relaxed and the muscles along his jaw unclenched. "Good. I'm asking."

"I'll get right on it. As soon as I'm back from my manicure appointment." She popped a few marshmallows into her mouth and grabbed for her purse. "Ta ta."

Annabelle emerged two hours later from the beauty salon feeling like a brand-new woman. She found Wag waiting for her behind her desk, wearing her telephone headset and lying.

"No, Mr. Achrom is not in. He's left for the day on a family emergency." Wagner punched at a few buttons on the phone. "Damn, cut them off again."

She smiled. "I didn't realize you had any family."

Wag looked up. He ripped the headset from his head, ruffling his brown hair in the process. "Where have you been? The phone has been ringing like crazy."

"Well, I was just going in to have my nails done, but I decided to have a partial day of beauty. You know, facial, massage."

Frustration and irritation flashed across his face. "No, I don't know. I do know I've been sitting at this desk for two hours now, probably scaring off business with every call."

Annabelle laughed and patted his smooth cheek, her new nails a sharp contrast. "I'm sure you weren't that bad."

Sidling around him, she brushed against his broad back. He'd taken off his suit coat, something he rarely did. The clearly defined muscles of his back rippled under his black shirt as he moved out of her way. She checked the urge to touch him, but her lips burned as she remembered their kiss this morning. This playing with fire appeared to have some disadvantages. Some delicious disadvantages.

"Are you wearing tennis shoes?" he asked.

She looked down at her skirt, bare legs and new running shoes. "I bought them right after the massage. I was so relaxed I couldn't imagine getting back into heels."

"But what about the office dress code?"

"Oh, I didn't tell you? I changed that this morning. I've instituted a casual workplace wardrobe. Since I'm not only the administrative assistant but also the office manager and bookkeeper, I had a conference with myself and made the new policy. I know how much you value order and efficiency, so I typed up the new procedures and put it on the minifridge in the breakroom."

Wag balanced himself on the edge of her desk, his innate formality vanished. She'd never seen his back anything other than ramrod straight. Doing something as casual as balancing on a desk was way out of the ordinary. She admired the play of muscles under his slacks.

"Besides, I hate panty hose. What a wasteful article of clothing that is. What are they supposed to look like anyway? Your skin. Isn't that ridiculous? I have skin. Why do I need to buy something that looks like skin to cover skin?"

Wag just nodded.

She never knew being naughty was so much fun. Missing a day of work, a real manicure and...oh! Had she discussed semi-intimate apparel with Wag? Her stomach tightened in embarrassment even as a strange, yet not unfamiliar, voice in her mind said, "Yeah, so what?"

She hoisted her leg on the desk. "Look at my leg. There's nothing wrong with it. It's a very serviceable leg. It gets me where I need to go."

When was the last time she felt so light and teasing? Not since high school, before she'd painfully learned just how dangerous the impulsiveness she'd inherited from her father could be.

He leaned forward and she sucked in a quick breath. She hadn't been so near to his face since the morning she woke up on his couch.

And this morning when she'd kissed him.

Right now the most gorgeous expression of confusion crossed his rugged features. He embodied the perfect picture of male bewilderment, from his ruffled hair to his unevenly aligned tie.

"Go home. Get some sleep. Don't return to the office until the old you is back."

She swallowed. Every nerve in her body danced. All the pent-up desire and emotion she'd felt for this man demanded she stand up, plant a kiss on him that he'd never forget, then walk out the door and find a man who'd appreciate her.

Annabelle had never listened to those feelings before. Maybe she should.

Maybe she shouldn't.

Angling her head, she smiled. Wag's beautiful blue eyes narrowed.

She licked her lips as his eyes drifted to her breasts. Belle spotted the male hunter's appreciation in the depths of his blue eyes and couldn't wait for his hands to stroke her there.

Kissing Wagner Achrom again went against every hard lesson she'd learned since her father's arrest and she'd started fighting against temptations toward impulsiveness. She'd never realized how much she'd missed in life until this very moment. But she didn't plan to miss anymore. Not today anyway.

Anticipation mingled with her impatience. Smiling, she ran her bright red, femme-fatale fingertips down the center of his tie.

"Do you? Do you really want the old Annabelle Scott back?"

An odd, almost wicked gleam entered his eyes.

STIFF KISSER.

Ms. Scott's accusation strangled him tighter than the threat of bankruptcy. *That* was the loss of money. Broke, he'd been there before. More than once. But this, *this* was a challenge of skill.

A test he'd passed since he was fifteen. With amazing scores.

He didn't expect to fail now. They'd get this stiff-kisser indictment resolved. Immediately.

No one had ever challenged him in the bedroom. Or at a desk, for that matter. Something heated and primal unfurled in his chest. The muscles of his neck and shoulders tightened.

Stiff kisser. He'd show her stiff. And they'd both enjoy it.

Once he'd proven her wrong, and he would, then he could get some productive work done. When he'd opened this office, the place had been a bustle of activity. Flush from his liquidation of stock options and cash out of his bonus packages, he'd taken on an accountant, a research assistant—even an intern for a few weeks.

Now all those employees were long gone, his current office space a fraction of what it used to be. Only that multiline telephone and Annabelle remained. He hated the damn phone, but Annabelle... His only true assets were his patents and Ms. Scott. And he valued her way too much. No.

No, he didn't need to destroy all he had left simply to prove he was still a man to fear. He'd made enough mistakes in his life. Taken enough risks. And this merger was the biggest gamble of his life.

Sure, he was no stranger to insolvency. Before he hit his stride as a venture capitalist, there'd been many a night of eating nothing but ramen noodles. When he'd lived in the apartment with no working stove, he'd eaten them cold and dry. But he had no intention of returning to that state any time soon. He needed a clear head and a clearheaded Annabelle. There would be no kissing.

"You didn't answer my question," Annabelle reminded him.

"Do I want the old Ms. Scott back?"

For a moment, the naughty glint in her brown eyes faded, leaving her appearing almost vulnerable. Something in that question, and the wealth of meaning he sensed resting behind her words when she'd prompted him, moved him.

"I liked the old Annabelle."

"You did?"

She sounded surprised. Annabelle dropped her gaze for a moment and rocked from foot to foot. She took a deep breath. Then she lifted her head. The naughty glint had returned, demanding and bright in her eyes.

"Are you going to like this new Annabelle?" she asked. "I do. She has a lot more fun."

Hell, maybe *he* needed a doctor. Or maybe this was how all men met their downfall. A slow, headlong fall into insanity. He could resist all kinds of temptation, but not the challenge issued by Ms. Annabelle Scott. Hell, as long as he was going to make a mistake…

He met her eyes. "That depends on whether you're going to grab my tie again or not."

4

THE HUNTED HAD BECOME the hunter.

Wagner had decided to play along.

Desire heated her blood. Annabelle's nose captured the scent of Wag's cologne, an artful blend of citrus and cedar that always made her toes curl in the morning as he passed her desk. How many days had she spent at her desk chair hoping he'd pass by so she'd smell that special scent of his mingled with the heat of his skin and his own natural musk. Mmm.

He stood behind her; the warmth of his breath teasing the sensitive skin of her neck, reawakening a fresh wave of desire.

His very body was an arsenal against any woman's defenses. Good thing she had no plans to resist. However, she was the one supposed to be in charge. A simple kiss should turn the tables back to her favor.

"Are you going to grab it? It's silk, but if you have to, I understand," Wagner said in a tone of mock pain.

Annabelle tilted her head, outraged. "Grab your tie? Certainly not. The tie was this morning's shtick. This is this afternoon's."

Man, oh man. She sure wasn't acting like herself. Well, not the self she'd been since leaving high school behind. That Annabelle focused on bills, college credits and repaying her aunt and uncle. But being the spontaneous Belle had its advantages. One she would exercise right now.

Belle angled toward him, grabbed him by the belt with both hands, jerked him toward her and crushed his lips to hers. He needed no second urging, his tongue moving along the seam of her lips. *Good.* She liked her men ready.

Wag's touch was a sheer assault on her senses. His lips, firm yet soft, traced along her mouth. He then gently nipped her lower lip, sucking the sensitive skin into his warm mouth. Soon he had her moaning deep in her throat. This kissing-yet-not-kissing thing he had going was far more sensual than anything she'd imagined even in her most daring daydreams.

The blinds were up, the door possibly unlocked. Anyone could walk in. Who cared? She liked being naughty to him.

Naughty was good. Wicked and, oh, so delicious.

Belle arched toward him, drawing him closer as she draped her arms around his neck. Wag's hands cupped her bottom and pulled her tight against him. His tongue traced the seam of her lips, compelling her to open her mouth to him again.

He was anything but stiff this time. Well, stiff only where it counted.

Feeling the hardness of his body against her own softer curves created a surge of warm, wet desire between her legs. Why'd she ever think Wagner would deliver a simple kiss? She'd challenged his skill this morning. Now he had something to prove. A complex man like Wag would be determined to show her every hot trick just to prove his skill.

He hadn't even fully kissed her yet and she was already crazy with wanting. Being in his arms felt so good. So right.

A delicious ripple of sensation followed the path Wag's hand took from her bottom, along her hip, lightly against her rib cage.

She couldn't breathe.

Her nipples tightened, craving his touch.

Longing for his hands, rough and thorough on her body, she grew aggravated at his slowness. Was it deliberate? A technique to build the excitement?

She didn't care. It was action time. Annabelle clasped Wag's hand and dragged it to her breast.

"Touch me here," she said against his lips, her voice sounding ragged and raw.

His other hand followed and Wag swallowed her gasp of pleasure as his hands cupped her breasts. Man, oh man, he was skilled. He kissed her fully, moving his tongue along hers.

She hugged his knee between her legs, pulling him closer. His hands caressed and stroked her breasts, but only through her clothes, heightening her frustration.

"You taste so good," he groaned against her mouth.

His words set her on fire. Belle wanted to be closer. Needed to be closer. Skin to skin.

For the moment, her body attuned itself to Wag's expert strokes with his hands, lips and tongue. Just like his business plans, his lectures on supply and demand, he left nothing to chance, monitored every detail. He gave her just enough supply to demand more. Every part of her body became a potential pleasurable target for his unique sensual onslaught.

The sound of staccato knocking on the front door was quickly followed by the rattling of the knob. Annabelle broke the kiss and ran her lips to his ear, tracing the sexy curve with her tongue. She planned to ignore whoever was at the door. Planned to ignore a lot of things. Everything but her desire.

Wag apparently planned to ignore the knocking, too. He hauled her flush against him, causing the pleasurable crush of her breasts against the firm, muscular hardness of his chest.

The beginning notes of Beethoven's Fifth signaled someone was trying to reach her on her cell. But it made only a slight dent in her concentration on his ear. She intended to nibble his lobe until her voice mail took over.

"Belle, it's Katie!" Her best friend's shout was muffled by the door. "Open up. I know you're still at work. I saw your car in the lot."

Trepidation filled her, pushing some of her heated desire to the side. *No. She didn't want to talk to Katie.*

"It's important—I've been trying to say something to you all day. If you don't pick up the phone or answer this door, I'm going to assume you're in there unconscious and I'm calling the police.

Her phone rang again. With a heavy sigh, she snatched her cell off her waistband. It had been poking her anyway. "Katie, I'm alive but busy. Can't talk right now," her voice more breath than substantive words.

"Just give me a second. About Thursday night, something happened at the par—"

Grabbing Wag by the belt again, Annabelle held the phone away from her ear. "Just can't spare the time. I'll call you later." She pressed the end button, then tossed the phone onto the carpeted floor. She didn't want to hear what Katie had to say, but that didn't mean she had to let go of his belt buckle. A girl had priorities.

The sound of their rough breathing meshed with the light blowing of the air conditioner. She met his gaze. His eyes blazed a deep indigo blue. He leaned forward for another kiss, but she shifted away.

"Much better than this morning," she told him. Time to shift this lovemaking back to her favor.

His gaze traveled down her body, lingering on the arousal of her breasts. "Based on your reaction, I'd say it was a hell of a lot better."

Shoving a stapler out of the way with her elbow, Annabelle reclined against the desk, balancing herself on her arms. She wanted him, but she couldn't make this too easy on him.

"What are you doing?" he asked.

"I'm waiting for you to launch the next strike. I was just getting used to that thing you did with your hands."

He raised an eyebrow. "Am I supposed to chase you around the desk?"

She gave him a slow, sexy smile. "Oh, now that's a very appealing fantasy. One I've had quite a few times."

The hot desire etched on his face suddenly turned cold as he backed away a step and adjusted his tie. "You have? That makes things a lot more interesting."

Okay, that sounded like a come-on, but why was he backing away? "How?"

"Are you still my employee?"

She nodded, a wave of unease dampening her passion. "Until the Anderson merger."

"Then our mutual fantasies will remain that. Fantasies." Wagner adjusted his tie into a perfect knot and smoothed one small wrinkle that dared to mar his shirt. "Good night, Ms. Scott."

Slowly, Annabelle straightened and smoothed her skirt down over her bare knees. The door clicked silently behind Wagner as he closed it.

Heat from waning desire and maybe even a little embarrassment warmed her cheeks. *This* was not how her seduction plan was supposed to work out. Okay, not that she had a plan, more of a spontaneous going-with-the-gut instinctual sort of strategy, but lying on her desk, hot, wet, bothered and *alone* had never entered her mind.

Speaking of minds, Wagner thought way too much. That was his problem. She wouldn't make that mistake again. The next time, and she *would* make a next time happen, there would be no thinking on his part. No stopping. No matter what.

Wait a second…had he said mutual?

Annabelle scooted off her desk, excitement making her fingers tingle. He had. He'd said mutual. For a moment, she reveled in the knowledge. So, Mr. Wagner Achrom hadn't been immune after all. In fact, she practically had a dent in her thigh from his erection.

Hmm, she needed a handful of marshmallows to think this thing through. Yanking open her bottom drawer, she surveyed the selection. Marshmallow trees covered in green sugar enticed her to strip open the cellophane packaging. At least something was stripping. Since the little trees were only available around Christmas, she'd been saving this particular treat for a special occasion. But this was really a tree-sugar moment.

And she needed a list.

Reaching under her large desk calendar she pulled out her notebook. Funny, she'd forgotten to mark the last day off with a meticulous straight line. Blast, she hated being so unspontaneous and unoriginal as marking the date off a calendar. But Wagner Achrom was a stickler for detail. Today she'd just have to make it a squiggly line. In magenta.

That task complete, she opened her notebook to a fresh page. The impression marks of her pen crossing through her mantras from the days before was clearly visible. That's what she needed. A new mantra. She'd start with the obvious.

Make Wag beg.

Hmm. She didn't really have any points after that. So many options. Panties or no panties? Finger foods or finger licking? It didn't matter. Her determination would not falter. "Tomorrow, Wag, those fantasies become reality."

WHAT THE HELL had happened?

And more importantly, why in the hell had he kissed Annabelle? Ms. Scott. He straightened his tie. Definitely Ms. Scott. Thinking of her as Annabelle was the last thing he needed. That made her seem less an assistant and more of a woman. A beautiful woman who made his mouth water.

Wagner pushed to his feet, his chair ricocheting off the credenza. He had a merger to amalgamate. Everything depended on its success. His business. His reputation. His promises to his mother as he'd stood beside her hospital bed and later his promises to himself to be proud of the man he'd become.

But that still didn't answer the question why he had kissed Annabelle? *Ms.* Annabelle Scott.

Scratch that. The why was obvious. Those "come kiss me" eyes, her "wrap your fingers in me" hair. The way she made pink seem anything but innocent. Although, like an idiot, the answer hadn't been obvious until a few hours ago.

With steady movements, he twisted the air-conditioning knob to high. Then he pushed up the window. He needed the heavy-duty cooling that only a brisk December gust could provide. Or a night in a willing woman's arms.

Annabelle's arms.

Damn. *Don't go there.*

He was messing up.

And he never messed up.

But he'd miscalculated with Ms. Scott. A miscalculation he couldn't afford. He despised not being able to concentrate on the goal, despised desiring someone more than common sense. His mother had suffered from that same malady until she'd finally left his dad. Great. He'd inherited both his parents' weaker points.

He wanted to chase.

Chasing Ms. Scott around the desk, crashing her files, telephone and pens to the floor, then driving her wild…damn.

Annabelle.

He allowed himself to think of her that way for just one moment, rolling the name around in his head. It had a sort of lilting, soothing quality. He yearned for a little something soft. A little something like Annabelle.

Hell, he'd even buy long and sell short for a taste of her sweet body.

That kiss, Annabelle's response. It'd be worth it. Remembering how right her breasts felt in his hands, how welcoming her mouth, her body…damn, it would have to be the cold shower.

Fantasies of Annabelle on the desk would have to wait. The deal with Anderson had to come first. Damn, why'd it have to be called a merger? He'd like to merge something and it wasn't companies and assets.

Personal interests could never win out over professional business. Never. His goals, that was all that mattered. Stalking to the safe, he punched in the code and yanked out the box holding his fuel-cell prototypes.

After only a few seconds in the dim light of his office, his new solar cell converted and banked enough energy to fuel a laptop for days. And that was just carrying it from his safe to his desk. Anderson wanted his silicon solar-cell-replacement technology to light up and power every remote farm and isolated home. Anderson could have his big gun, but he wouldn't allow them to gain control of his fuel cell.

Wagner positioned the cell toward the window. Light from the sun, a lamp, even a campfire would make this baby zoom with power. *This* would be his.

Popping open the protective casing, Wagner inspected the seam. He was close. So close to making this deal. No more peanut butter and jelly or three-cans-for-a-dollar tuna. He'd not only reclaim his old life of luxury, but exceed it. Prove to all the critics who laughed at his attempts to succeed on new terms—who said he was only a destroyer, a player, never a builder—that he was more.

So much more.

But if he didn't get cash influx now, it would all be over. He'd fail...just like his father.

First he had to make all the dominoes fall into place. And signing this deal with Anderson without giving away the right to the cell in his hand was the first domino to fall. He wouldn't raze his chances when he was only inches away from success.

Wager examined the inside, searching for corrosion. He found none. But deterioration could be tricky to find. No one looking at his parents' marriage would have seen the erosion. His mother had been hurt time and time again by his father's failed ventures and dealings. But the world saw a fully charged unit.

Walking away from the hospital after his mother died, Wagner had vowed never to put someone through the living hell his father had put his family through. His mother had lost everything she'd ever worked for supporting a man whose pipe dreams never became more than that.

He'd learned something today. Annabelle was the type to demand he notice her. In and out of the bedroom. But he wouldn't do it. His promise pounded his thoughts, reminding him he'd not seek a relationship until he had financial security and regained what he'd lost when he'd walked away from the corporate raider game five years ago.

He was here to play by his own rules. But right now, his own goals and future stretched before him

still out of reach. Any woman, especially Annabelle,
deserved more. So much more.

Definitely Ms. Scott.

DAMN. His eyes strayed again. And here, like an idiot,
Wagner had congratulated himself on only allowing
his eyes to stray to Ms. Scott's breasts once. She sat,
mere yards away in the outer office, but with the al-
lure of her lush body heavy on his mind, she might
as well be sitting in his lap.

Adjusting the thermostat so she didn't get chilled
had been a stroke of genius. But those bare feet of
hers, and the crazy way she'd painted her toenails,
made him wonder what other daring things lay just
below the surface. Like, was she wearing a bra? One
of those Wonder thingies? Just a glimpse of her de-
sirably full breasts peeking out of her low-cut blouse
made him sweat.

Damn. Third time his gaze strayed to her breasts.

She didn't arch and sigh the way she did last
week. Instead, Annabelle simply reclined, looking
graceful and natural. And arousing as hell.

To think he'd expected to get a little work done
today. Yesterday was a total write-off. Except for
that kiss.

And Annabelle's reaction.

He'd never kissed, merely kissed, a woman and
felt such a link, such a total meshing of desires.

Work.

But as soon as the merger finalized, he'd find

Annab—Ms. Scott a new job and then the seduction market would be open for business. And he'd indulge in every fantasy…

And he'd also annihilate the trust and respect he saw in Annabelle's eyes by involving her in a going-nowhere affair, destined to fail. And it would fail. Every woman he'd ever been with possessed a very similar inventory of his "lack ofs"—lack of sharing, lack of communication, lack of…

He didn't know what was going on in Ms. Scott's head, but he knew she was, what was it…*a nice girl.*

What a corny, old-fashioned phrase. But until yesterday, she was the poster girl for that particular term. And what's more…he liked her that way. Although he liked her this way, too, but he wouldn't disrespect the only person in the world to believe he deserved even a modicum of faith.

But what the hell had happened to Ms. Scott? His mind replayed their past encounters, the parts where they weren't kissing, to search for clues. The picnic. The day he first noticed her in that clingy sweater. She'd wanted to celebrate her graduation. Maybe the change in Ms. Scott could be attributed to just a simple case of no-more-responsibility-itus. And who was he to ruin the party?

His elbow slipped and the lead snapped from the metal tip of his mechanical pencil.

Work. Desk. Contract. Pencil. Concentrate.

But that damn desk taunted him. Actually, it was laying Annabelle back on the desk that taunted him.

He could still picture her on top of it, her panties peeking from under her skirt.

Annabelle was wreaking havoc with his business plan and giving him a lesson in supply and demand. She'd planted that image of him chasing her around the desk. And getting caught.

She definitely looked ready to run. The most impractical pair of shoes lay in a discarded heap at her feet. If you could even call a heeled sole and two thin pieces of leather straps shoes.

On the other hand, those leather straps looped about her delicate ankle and glided up her calf, conjuring thoughts of her body, Annabelle wearing leather. And taking it off. Slowly.

Her red-tipped, pink-striped toenails curled into the carpet, like those of a woman seeking all the pleasure the senses provided. Would her fingers curl just as easily along his body?

His blood heated.

He was messing up again. Damn.

She turned to face him. Her dark brown eyes, and the secret smile tugging at her full bottom lip, let him know she'd caught him staring. Her slender fingers stroked along her calf the way a lover would. His eyes followed her every movement as she caressed her foot.

"Do you like it?" she asked.

Oh, yeah.

"It's called Persuasion."

"What?"

She wiggled her tempting little toes at him. "My nail polish. It's called Persuasion."

"What about the stripes?"

"That's a technique one of my friends taught me. She says it never fails to grab a man's attention. She calls it 'take me now toes.'"

Her friend was dangerous.

"She's given me a few more hints on how to bring a man to his knees."

Annabelle dropped her feet to the carpet and padded barefoot to him. Soundless. Slow and sensual, like a prowling tigress.

"Ann—Ms. Scott, I don't have time to chat—I have work to do."

She leaned against the door frame, one red-tipped, pink-striped toe crossing the threshold, playing with the carpet. The skirt she wore ruffled at the end, playing with the skin of her thighs.

How easy it would be to stand, walk to her and draw her into his arms. To learn with his fingers and lips if she wore a bra or not. To drive out the burning need to make her his.

"All work and no play makes Wag a very dull boy."

Dull? He had an erection that could drive a spike through steel. "I, uh, need some time alone."

"I'll shut your door, but first, I plan to introduce a little play into your life."

He had to get her out of there. But the need to know her plans rooted him to the spot. "How do you plan to do that?"

Annabelle's fingers played with the gathered material of her skirt, lifting it an inch. Just enough to tantalize. "By letting you know I'm not wearing any panties. Don't forget, I rescheduled your meeting with Smith and Dean in an hour." And with a drop of her ruffle and a wink, Annabelle closed the door behind her.

SCREW MUSING about the uncertainty of whether or not Annabelle wore a bra. That was the least of his worries. Now he knew for certain she wore nothing below that tight, red skirt with that taunting little ruffle.

He almost stalked after her. What the hell would he do with her if he caught her? Shove his potential second chance through the glass window. He already didn't care he'd scattered half the file to the floor.

Instead, he shifted uncomfortably in his chair.

Dammit. Smith and Dean in an hour. How could he play hardball when he was so har—

Bending, he shuffled his papers into a stack and stuffed them into his briefcase. He'd walk to Smith and Dean's office. The brisk pace might exhaust his libido.

Straightening his tie, he strode into the outer office where he immediately spotted his assistant with her legs stretched out and crossed at the ankle. Not primly tucked beneath the desk.

Ms. Scott had great legs. His glance followed the line of her body. Great everything.

Business. Impersonal.

"Please call Smith and Dean and let them know I'm on my way over."

"Happy to oblige," she said, uncrossing her legs. *I'm not wearing any panties.*

That little taunt fogged his brain.

Damn. He'd have to jog to Smith and Dean's office and work up a sweat just to cool himself off.

With a nod, he stalked to the elevator, jabbing the down button. Yeah, if only it could be that easy. After twenty floor dings, he stepped out into the bustling lobby of the Morris Building. Women in suits and sneakers and men in business casual filed around him to step onto the elevator. Leaving the glass-and-steel structure, he joined the crowd on the sidewalk.

This was normal.

The hustle of the city.

The anonymity of the crowd.

The smell of deals in the air.

Not miniskirt-wearing assistants. Not a steady receptionist who grabbed him by the tie. Not a woman whose professionalism had been replaced with irreverence. And what was with the marshmallows?

Limbo. He hated limbo. His professional life was in limbo and now the one area, the one person he could count on, had become tantalizingly…and frustratingly unpredictable. Wagner picked up his pace, briskly navigating among the downtown Oklahoma City workers leisurely strolling on this springlike winter day.

When he came back from this meeting, they'd have a face-to-face where he'd simply outline the terms of appropriate office behavior and his expectations.

That settled, Wagner forced himself to stop thinking about Annabelle for now. He had to steel himself for the feeding frenzy to come. And he was the minnow. Argus Smith and Raymond Dean were the CEO and CFO of the Anderson Group, two of the most loathsome businessmen Wagner had ever faced off against.

He detested Smith the most. Argus Smith had had the pleasure of turning down Wagner's father for investment capital time and time again. Although he had to hand it to old man Smith. He'd waited the game out. Now, with little more than chump change, he'd gain access to the Achrom patents he'd tried to weasel from Wagner's father.

It had given Wagner intense satisfaction to best Smith several years ago. The first holding Wagner had ever wrested from an unsuspecting board of directors belonged to Smith. Though it had proved to be only a small satisfaction for Smith's breaking of his old man's heart and dreams over and over. And his mother's.

Wagner didn't hold all the cards in this match, but he could still play an ace. And bluffing was an essential part of the game.

After a buzz on the administrative assistant's desk, she ushered Wagner into the empty conference room. A negotiation trick. He'd used it himself...to unnerve his competitors as their anxiety grew the longer they waited.

Conference rooms, boardrooms, *here* Wagner felt comfortable. In control. Not like his own office across town.

They'd try to weasel; he'd prevent it. Par for the business course.

Ten minutes later, Smith and Dean arrived. After a round of handshakes, they sat down along the cherry-wood conference table. After he declined coffee, the administrative assistant shut the massive doors behind her.

White folders lay in front of them. An extra folder lay before an empty chair across from him.

He indicated the folder with an uplifted eyebrow.

"Someone may be joining us later," Smith said, his tone evasive.

Irritation filled him. The man was up to something. Wagner prepared himself, making sure he appeared cool and assured. He was the last to open his prospectus. *Yeah, he didn't care if they signed on the red line or not.* Image was everything.

Fifteen minutes later, Dean handed him a cigar. "Nice to have you on board with Anderson, Wagner. Almost."

Almost? They were about to sign off on the deal. Where the hell did this come from? Wagner stuffed the cigar into his suit pocket.

"Achrom Enterprises will be an asset to the Anderson family. You've had a nice little run on your own," Dean rambled on.

"Except you've been funding your new business primarily through an increase in debt," Smith said, his deep guffaw causing his belly to shake.

Wagner resisted his urge to reply sharply and instead offered the two men a polite smile. Nice case of good cop, bad cop. One would hit him with the condescending "we're proud of you" while the other socked him in the gut with an insult.

And there was something still to come. He knew the signs. Wayne lifted his glass. "And now your money, Smith. Much like how I financed my first takeover of…one of your companies, right?"

Smith's eyes narrowed, but he laughed just the same before he took a drink from his own glass. The two could and would throw every curve they had at him. There'd be no hard feelings. It wasn't personal…just business.

Dean clapped his hands together and focused his attention on Wagner. "How do you plan to spend your money?"

"Oh, I have a few ideas." *No way.* He knew this tactic, too. Wagner didn't plan to reveal his ideas and see Anderson Group reap the benefits. "And you?" he asked.

The opening of the conference-room door interrupted Smith's next words. His lips twisted into a smile as the assistant ushered in a newcomer. Ah, the last folder now had an owner. Damn. Wagner had enjoyed toying with Smith, nearly making him lose his edge.

With an unhurried twist of the head, Wagner turned his attention onto the newcomer. He looked vaguely familiar, but then the Oklahoma City business community was a small one. Rich and powerful from its influx of oil and gas money, but still small enough to recognize most of the players.

Smith cleared his throat. "Meet Kenny Rhoads."

Rhoads. Ah, a familiar last name. He was a lobbyist with strong ties to both Oklahoma politics and business. Rhoads didn't extend his hand. Neither did Wagner. So that was how it was to be. Why the hell was he here?

Smith leaned back in the conference-room chair, the hinges creaking under his weight. Wagner spotted the cold, assessing glances passing between him and Rhoads. He sensed a heightened level of excitement in Smith. This was not good. The bad blood between them probably made this deal a mighty hard agreement to take. No one had signed. Plenty could still go wrong.

Smith wanted to see him squirm.

Wagner chose not to give him the satisfaction.

"Mr. Rhoads has joined us as another interested party," Dean finally said.

Rhoads glanced down at the folder before him but didn't open it. "You brokered quite a deal here, Achrom. That reputation of yours is well earned."

Wagner said nothing. He didn't like the man, nor

his tone, but he kept his expression neutral. *Don't give anything away.* A lesson his father never learned. Rhoads drummed his fingers on the table, leaving small smears on the high-polished veneer. He didn't like the play. Something about Rhoads triggered his apprehension.

Rhoads's fingers stilled and a snide smile pulled at the corners of his lips. "But the deal's lost if the House doesn't pass the pending farm bill." His eyes narrowed. "Your whole future rides on that bill."

Wagner shrugged. "That bill will provide millions of dollars for farmers across the country to invest in solar-funded projects. Those patents hold the power to do everything from heating farmhouses to pumping water from wells."

Wagner knew it could be revolutionary. A boon to every rural area not only in the United States but across the world.

Finally, Rhoads opened the folder before him, but he never glanced down. "I have it on good authority that bill's going nowhere."

He didn't have time to school his features. He glanced toward Smith and Dean. "You'll back out of our agreement if the bill doesn't pass?"

Rhoads leaned forward. "Without the funding that bill would provide, Anderson would take on too much risk liability by developing the product without guaranteed profits."

"Hell, almost every new venture starts without guaranteed profits." He'd planned on his cut of the profits to pay for his own ideas. A risk, but that's the way business worked.

Dean simply shrugged. "It's outlined in the amendment we messengered over twenty minutes ago."

"I'd already left the office." To work off his sexual frustration in order to concentrate on this merger.

"Yes, your assistant mentioned that."

And they didn't bother to fill him in upon his arrival. How convenient. How shrewd.

He met Smith's and Dean's eyes, never wavering. "We have an agreement. A well-negotiated one." He allowed the warning behind his words hang in the air. If they wanted to renegotiate, he'd work it to *his* advantage.

"I know a few of your creditors…" Rhoads let his words trail, an implied threat.

Wagner surged to his feet. "You son of a—" He bit back the rest of his words. Now he knew their game. Use the power behind the Rhoads name to stall the congressional bill he was depending on for revenue. That was a particularly effective tactic to take away his potential earnings. Frustration drew his muscles taut. That agriculture bill was essential. He'd been counting on that legislation. By stalling the bill, Rhoads would destroy Wagner's only option to make his own way. Without the huge potential profits the bill would facilitate, he'd be sunk.

Kenny Rhoads was their hatchet guy.

Smith and Dean must have had a chance to study his financials. They realized he was on the brink of bankruptcy and figured if they strung him along with this ag bill, he'd fold. If the bill wasn't approved right away, he'd have no money to keep his company afloat. His creditors would sacrifice sell his assets, his father's patents—the very ones Anderson wanted—for a pittance. The Anderson Company could then pick up the leftover pieces of his company without the outflow of cash and Wagner to deal with day to day. All without having to get their hands dirty.

A nice little setup.

"That bill is a deal breaker. Your ideas will be useless to us without the funding available from that legislation. It goes to the House floor late this week if you're lucky. More likely early next week. Until then, we're in limbo."

He'd expected a promise and a handshake. Not string-alongs and veiled threats. More limbo. Screw limbo. He'd make that bill happen.

Rhoads lit up his cigar. "Until then, I'll be keeping my eye on you."

Wagner relaxed. This was his element. He'd dealt with wrenches in negotiations often. He held the upper hand. Anderson wanted what he had. His silicon solar-cell-replacement technology *was* the supply, which meant until he went bankrupt he held the control. And control was the name of the game. They wanted to play tough—well, he knew how to play rough.

ANNABELLE SHOVED the evidence of her marshmallow feast to the bottom drawer of her desk as Wagner walked through the door. Strain pulled at his eyes, the grooves along his lips were deeper with lack of sleep and fatigue. She'd almost feel sorry for him if she hadn't already planned to zap the rest of his energy on the couch of his office.

He'd been working too long on this merger and missed his last haircut. Not that she minded. The brown locks were longer than he usually wore them and the ends brushed against his shirt collar, curling a little.

The only part of him attesting to his past. His wayward side.

He obviously found the excessive length annoying, as he'd pushed his hair behind his ear. His ear was smooth and well formed, with an angle and a curve that drew her attention. A perfect ear. Of course, she couldn't see how Wagner Achrom would have anything on his body that wasn't perfect. It wouldn't be allowed. But it was sexy, too.

"You know, Wag, I've never particularly found ears sensual, but yours have a quality I can't quite define. I want to slide my tongue along the ridge, nibble on your lobe."

"Ms. Scott."

It was the tone. Something had happened in his meeting with Smith and Dean over at Anderson. Something not good. "What happened?"

"Nothing that can't be contained, but I need all the information you can get on a joint congressional bill between the Small Business Administration and the Department of Agriculture."

"What's going on?"

"Hardball. There's a bill in committee that would allocate money to rural communities developing alternative sources of power and to the companies that develop those sources."

"Isn't that just the kind of thing Anderson wants to develop with your patents?"

"Precisely."

"So what's the problem?"

"From what I've been able to piece together since my meeting with Smith and Dean—politics. At the urging of Ke—er, another interested party, a few representatives on the committee have tacked on some amendments that others in the committee find distasteful. Now the bill is stalled with some Congress members refusing to vote. I need to understand who these representatives are and what I can use to rally support around this bill."

"Right away. I'm assuming this is a rush job," she said, leaning forward.

Wagner nodded, his gaze darting to her cleavage, then back to her eyes. Those glances gave him away. Oh, he presented refined, but behind the stuffed and pressed shirt, he was raw.

"Back to the business model?" she asked. Wagner had drilled the Achrom business model into her head. Companies usually grew one way or another. Through debt, always a risk, but a widespread practice. Or the acquiring of other smaller companies at an even greater risk.

Wagner opposed takeovers.

And if he didn't get on with the business of her, she'd design a takeover of her own. Pushing away from her chair, she propped her hip against her desk. Wariness entered his eyes, but he didn't back away. Good.

"May I suggest you consider the dreaded two-pronged approach?"

He raised an eyebrow. "Acquisition."

"Hmm."

"Why do I get the impression you're not taking my business concerns seriously?"

Annabelle reached to straighten Wagner's tie. That should make him more comfortable. The backs of her fingers grazed the warm skin above his collar.

"Oh, I take it very seriously. You taught me all I know about supply and demand. Maybe it's time you created a little bit of demand."

"Thank you, Ms. Scott, I'll, uh take that under advisement."

Wagner shot into his office. Damn. Was that conversation out there about business? And had she been reading his mind?

Demand.

Ms. Scott created a lot of demand. Yeah, she knew the plan well, although he didn't think he'd taught her. She'd created the demand. She also maintained supply.

But she also had a point.

Okay, so maybe his business plan needed a little reworking. Perhaps he could have his merger and Annabelle, too. A two-pronged approach, all right. Business and fun. Hell, it wouldn't have bothered him five years ago. But even as he played with this option, a nagging twinge of guilt resurfaced.

Annabelle and the frustration she created had his gut twisting in knots. He couldn't think straight. Couldn't manage his business. He'd come in worried about the bill, creditors and this merger. Now she had him thinking business plans and mergers of a different kind.

His body hardened.

If he didn't do something soon about her, he'd lose his mind and his business. And at this point, he couldn't pinpoint which was more important.

What the hell had happened to his pledge of non-involvement with Annabelle Scott? The oath that stated he was a class-A son of a bitch and didn't mess with women who didn't know the score?

Apparently, Annabelle had learned a few things. Grab-you-by-the-balls-and-not-let-go kind of things. And she seemed perfectly healthy. In fact, Annabelle was a very healthy woman, rounded and curved in all the right places. Whatever strange flu that made her walk around barefoot and grab him by the belt, he'd caught. The thought of losing his shirt didn't scare him the way it had a week ago. In fact, it would just make getting naked with Annabelle that much easier.

And he was damn nuts.

Yeah, he'd caught something all right. Insanity.

Supply and demand.

And based on the uncomfortable tightness in his pants, he wouldn't be able to treat this particular malady until he'd taken a little bit of the cure only Annabelle could provide.

Yes, he was sick. What kind of sick idiot would turn down a hot night with a beautiful, fun, willing woman in his arms? *Could* turn Annabelle down.

Somewhere between this morning and this afternoon, he'd lost control. And he never lost control.

And he wouldn't start now.

Focus.

Identify the enemy. Smith and Dean were out solely for the biggest buck at the cheapest price. Not really personal. But Kenny Rhoads…the man was a shark. The man's name nagged at him. The nagging intensified when he entered the office and Annabelle greeted him with a smile and invitation. And he didn't want her to know the man's name. Why?

Rotating in his chair, he yanked open the file drawer in his desk. Inside he found Annabelle's personnel file, complete with background check. He scanned the pages until he found the information he sought. Satisfied his instincts were right, he replaced the folder.

He'd seize the opportunity to confront the past as he set up this deal. Wagner had demons, not all his own, to exorcise. He welcomed the chance. Before this deal was through, Annabelle might just have to face the past her father left her.

Something strange surged through him, strengthening his resolve. What was the word for it... protectiveness?

No. There had to be another word. Now he was actually losing his skill at forming coherent thoughts.

Red pens, contracts and patent protection didn't seem nearly as important as chasing Annabelle around the desk. Supply and demand.

He wanted her. Damn, more than this merger?

Maybe it was time to find out. Straightening his tie, his new blue tie, Wag pressed the intercom button. Yeah, supply and demand.

"Yes?"

"Ms. Scott. Annabelle...I need you."

5

A SHUDDER OF DESIRE coursed through her entire body, delicious, wicked and heady. How long had she been waiting to hear Wag say those words?

Well, four years, but today she'd been waiting at least five minutes. Now she knew why the no-panty trick worked. A man couldn't keep his mind on anything else, the knowing but not seeing. But she had to give Wag credit. He'd lasted longer than she'd expected—a true testament to his incredible strength of will. A will she planned to smash into the plush beige carpet with her red-tipped, pink-striped toe.

She brushed a bit of pink sugar off her fingertips and grabbed her spiral notebook. She might as well look the part and pretend she thought he'd called her in to do some work.

Throwing back her shoulders and fluffing up her hair, she drew in a deep breath. Grabbing a handful of marshmallows, she walked to his office. She was ready. She'd been ready for four long years. She knocked on the door, then without waiting for a reply, turned the handle.

Wag sat behind his desk, his navy blue tie perfectly aligned. His back was ramrod straight. Excellent. He was at his most uptight. The sun blazed over his left shoulder, casting a shadow over the tautness of his skin and the not-a-hair-out-of-place head. But his blue eyes smoldered, watching her every step into the room.

This was it. His naughty downfall. Her nipples tightened against the softness of her cotton shirt, her breasts turning full and heavy.

Annabelle drew her toe along her leg, satisfaction making her strong and bold, as she saw Wag's gaze darken, linger on her toes and slide up to her ankles. His eyes continued to follow the path she started… even after she stopped.

"What did you need me for?" she asked, her voice husky, seductive. Annabelle rubbed a marshmallow along her lower lip. "I was just eating a marshmallow."

She flicked the tip of her tongue to the tasty treat. Wagner sucked in a breath. "Would you like one?" she asked.

Wagner shook his head.

"Did you want some coffee, perhaps?" Annabelle had been on a coffee-making strike since Wag made his first…and only pot…a few days ago.

She leaned toward him. "Remind me again, do you like it hot and sweet."

His lips twisted. "Are we talking about coffee?"

"If you want it quick, that's just the way I'll give it to you. We only have instant," she reminded him.

Poor Wag. Did he just gulp? Katie was right, the double entendre was a delightful art.

Then he leaned against his chair, straightening his tie. Silent. She almost physically felt his eyes stripping away her clothes, gauging whether her teasing promise could be true.

"With instant, the pleasure hits you the moment you bring it to your lips. But there's something to be said about anticipation."

He shook his head. "I'll take the quickie—instant will be fine," he said.

"I'll be happy to get it on." This seduction stuff grew easier by the minute. A flutter tightened her tummy.

Annabelle licked her lips, keeping her movements slow and deliberate.

"I don't want coffee," he growled.

A tense, but not uncomfortable, silence settled upon them, a prelude to what they both had to know was inevitable. Wag would be hers. But first he had some making up to do for all the years of ignoring her sensuality. Remember the mantra. *Make Wag Beg.*

She vamped to his desk.

"I have a confession to make," she said, standing beside him. "My toenail polish isn't really called Persuasion. I just said that to keep your mind off your manners."

He swallowed again, his gaze roaming down her bare legs to her toes. "What's it called?"

She shrugged, as she hopped onto the edge of his

desk, her red skirt riding high. "Oh, something boring. Fire-engine red."

Straddling her feet on the wooden armrests of his executive chair, she pushed him backward, the wheels gliding easily on the plastic mat. The powerful muscles under his jacket bunched. She couldn't wait to ogle that body of his.

He didn't look like a man upset about a name change. "Not very tempting."

"True. But what if I did something like this?" First, she wiggled her striped toes at him, then traced the line of Wag's leg with her toe, inching closer to his zipper.

"Maybe I should suggest my new nail-polish name to the manufacturers. Might raise their sales. You taught me all about supply and demand."

His fists clenched, then loosened. "I'd say it's time to douse the flames."

With a surge of male sexual frustration and strength, he pulled her into his lap. She landed against the hardness of his chest. Yearning, which seared beneath the surface, flared, turning her flushed and hungry.

Annabelle noticed his eyes first, full of fire and determination. An intense shade of blue. She'd become so used to Wag keeping himself in firm control, she'd forgotten his old reputation as an intimidating and calculating corporate raider. A man of power and force.

It was inevitable he'd lose control.

All that energy and strength he'd used to broker multimillion-dollar deals and corporate takeovers was now focused squarely on her. It was thrilling and unnerving at the same time. She curled her body toward his. The hardness of his powerful body pressed against her most sensitive places. She arched her hips, cupping him with her body. His answering groan was a sound she ached to wrench from him again and again.

She'd never want to see him any other way now: the real Wag, his body tensed with raw power.

His fingers caressed the bare skin above her knee. Oh, yeah, she knew what he was thinking. He had to find out for himself whether she really wasn't wearing panties. His questing fingers found the skirt's hem, brushing the soft material against her thighs.

"I want you naked, Annabelle."

She had trouble catching her breath. It was really going to happen. After all these long years of pent up desire and frustration, she was now finally going to make love to Wagner Achrom.

What was she waiting for? She didn't actually have to hear him beg.

She looked up, eye to eye with him. The central air unit kicked off and the sound of their increasingly ragged breathing filled the air. The warmth of his breath brushed her cheek. And the citrus cologne that never failed to drive her crazy had her leaning into his neck. She was close, but she wanted to be closer.

She tasted the skin of his neck with her tongue, drawing her tongue along his collarbone until she found his pulse. The rapid tempo of his heartbeat attested to his heightened need for her. Wag sucked in a breath, his hands cupping her bottom over her skirt, tugging her nearer. Mmm, she loved being nearer, as her own racing heartbeat demonstrated.

Wait a second. He was taking control again and this was her show. She planned to make this last. And there was something to be said about anticipation. She had four years to make up for. They both had a desk fantasy to realize.

Scrambling off his lap, she met his gaze. "Hmm, rather spontaneous of you, Mr. Achrom. I know you like to hunt. Why don't I let you chase me around your desk and when you catch me, I get to take one item of your clothing. Off."

He stood beside her, his full six feet plus towering above her. He smiled down at her. "Shouldn't I be the one taking off your clothing?"

She laughed deep in her throat. "Don't let me stand in your way."

With a light push to his shoulders, she was off. Laughing, she darted over to the far side of his desk.

A gleam entered the blue depths of his eyes, turning them the color of a darkening cloud, like the dangerous tornadoes that crossed the Oklahoma plains. Wagner looked every inch the ruthless man he'd claimed to be an hour ago. She shuddered in wanting, liked the danger element finally breaking through that oh-so-straight-tie-life he'd been lead-ing and that she was the one to help him crash through the barrier.

He moved toward her, his steps slow and deliber-ate, like a stalking tiger. His shoulder muscles bunched and released, his body turning fluid. His dark blue eyes never broke from her. She couldn't look away. Didn't want to. She took a step away, but he stalked closer.

When had she just thought of him as simply a stiff businessman? He was a hungry predator. A preda-tor prowling to mate. He trailed her around the desk, until only a breath separated them.

His hand, gentle and firm, encircled her arm. "Caught you."

She licked her lips. She reached for the material at his shoulders. "Yes, but I've caught you, too." She pushed the fine wool of his suit jacket past his shoul-ders and down. The soft material fell to the floor with a whoosh, sending a rush of cool air against her bare legs.

She lifted an eyebrow. "You going to pick that up and carefully drape it across the back of your chair?"

Wag didn't say a word. Instead, he traced his fin-gers up her forearm, over her biceps, to tease the bare skin at her shoulder. A wave of goosebumps fol-lowed the path of his tantalizing fingers.

He didn't say a word as his hand slipped under the silky material of her blouse, her skin tightening and aching for his touch.

And he didn't say a word as he dropped his hands after only a few seconds of his wonderful, thrill-stirring strokes.

"Are you going to chase me again?" she asked.

Wag shook his head. He clasped her hands in his and brought her fingers to the buttons of his shirt. Then, with her hands under his, he pulled his shirt apart, buttons flying.

"The games are over," he growled against her lips.

Yes, the games were over. Now it was time for some serious business. Wagner Achrom should fully understand that concept.

Her plans didn't include a sedate, button-by-button removal of his shirt. This would not be a one-foot-on-the-floor approach.

She yanked the oxford shirt from his pants, then ran her hand under the soft cotton of his T-shirt until she felt his skin. She stroked his taut abs, followed the trail of his sparse hair up his stomach to his deliciously hard chest. Yummy.

He felt so good. She didn't want to stop touching him. The tips of her fingers ached to caress along the smooth sinew of his back and her palms itched to run along the hard muscles of his shoulders. But she had to get closer. No longer content to touch under his shirt, she had to get it off. Now.

Annabelle grabbed the hem of his T-shirt and yanked it over his head. She had to see as well as feel the hot bare skin she'd exposed. The sight of him flooded her body with wild sensation.

Wag exhaled sharply as she placed a quick kiss on his chest. He cupped her breasts, her nipples tightening against the thin material of her shirt. Frustration at the barrier of her clothes sent a fiery punch to her blood.

With relief she felt his long fingers at the top of her shirt. Slowly he released the top pearl button. The cooler office air did nothing to relieve the heat of her skin. Why was he taking so long? She moaned deep in her throat as his lips found the sensitive skin at the base of her neck.

Annabelle arched toward him, urging him on. Finally he had the last button undone. Shrugging her shoulders, she flung her blouse to the corner of the desk.

His hand and mouth moved lower, to the skin he'd just uncovered. His touch wasn't gentle, but it wasn't rough. The embrace of a man who wanted. Wanted as desperately as she. The warmth of his breath teased the skin at her collarbone and then between her breasts.

Wag's hot, wet mouth on her breast sent a shudder of desire skittering through her body. It was too much and not enough at the same time. She arched to meet his hands and lips, her body rising from the smooth cool surface of his desk.

"Let's get out of here," he said against her breast, the heat from his breath sending another wave of sensation rippling through her.

"Where?"

"I don't care. Wait. Not my place."

Opening her eyes, she met the dark blue hue of his gaze. When had she ever thought his eyes resembled the coldness of a sapphire? Heat shot from those dark, luminous orbs.

Her blouse tossed to the ground, her skirt wadded up at her waist, her body aching with raw desire, Annabelle reached for him. The bulge under his pants sent a flooding warmth between her legs. Wagner Achrom wanted her. Bad.

He wanted to leave. Was he crazy? Shaking her head, she grasped one of his hands. "Here. We stay here." Her voice sounded husky, wanton to her own ears. She loved the sensation. Why hadn't she dared to seduce Wagner Achrom a long time ago?

"Here?" he asked.

Grabbing Wag by the shoulders, she hoisted herself up off the desk, straddling his lap. His eyes focused on the sway of her breasts.

"You have amazing breasts. I haven't been able to think of anything else."

"Show me what you wanted to do," she urged. Her nipples tightened harder in anticipation. She wanted to feel his hands on her body.

He cupped her breasts with both hands, her flesh spilling over. She closed her eyes and arched into his touch. His fingers shot pinpoint shocks of desire through her. For once she didn't mind the roundness of her body. Wag's eyes and lips didn't seem to care that her larger-than-average cup size prevented her from wearing some of the latest fashions.

She didn't think it possible, but the bulge nestling between her legs grew bigger. And harder. Touching the sensitive places between her legs. She rocked against him.

"Annabelle, you're killing me."

His words sounded teasing, but his manner spoke all business. A man who'd been pushed past his breaking point. Perfect.

She smiled at him. "I haven't even started." With another rock of her body against his, she leaned back, reaching for his belt. The cool clasp of metal holding his belt together gave way quickly under her fingers. A button and fly was all that prevented her from touching him. Holding him. Stroking him. Tasting him.

Instead, she simply rubbed her hand along the closed zipper. A deep groan rose from Wagner's gut.

"Do you like this?" She rubbed along the zipper again.

Wagner swallowed. "Yeah."

Mmm, hmm. Wagner never said words like *yeah*. He always said *yes*.

Lowering to her knees, she grabbed the zipper with her teeth. Wag groaned with each millimeter lower, his stomach growing taut. A slow torture. Perfect.

He wore boxers. Black silk. Ah, a touch of the carnally naughty. She loved a man who wore boxers. His erection pushed against the material. Pushing toward her.

She shoved his pants lower, kissing the sensitive skin of his inner thigh.

"Tell me what you want." She wanted to sound playful, but the words sounded wanton.

"You," he said on a groan.

Ah, now she could be playful. "Where…here? Or on the couch?" Ever since he'd woken her with the smell of coffee under her nose, she'd fantasized about him waking her up as she slept on the couch, but no coffee was involved. Only him. His lips. His hands. His body.

She gently placed a hand on the bulging material. Annabelle smiled as he flinched.

"Not the couch. Here," he said on a ragged breath. "Right here."

"Tell me. Tell me you want my mouth on your body."

Silence stretched between them.

In a sudden burst of movement, Wagner jerked her beside him on the desk, then covered her with his large body. "Not until you do."

His hands touched her everywhere. He was…frantic. Caressing her arms, tracing a path along her leg.

If he continued like this, *she* might be the one doing the begging.

His fingers teased her skin, closing in on her core. "I've been thinking about you all day. Whether you told the truth or not."

The charged fog swirling around her mind cleared a bit. "About what?"

"If you left your panties at home," he whispered in her ear, sending a shudder down her neck, along her back, settling between her legs.

"Did you want me to?"

His tongue flicked her earlobe. "There's something very satisfying about dragging a woman's panties down her legs. Feeling the contrast between hot, smooth skin and silky panties. You wouldn't wear cotton panties?"

"No. Never." She'd throw the whole drawerful of them away this very night.

He traced the curve of her ear with his tongue. "Since I can't slide my hands down your body, feeling your skin against silk, I think we'll just have to improvise."

She nodded…improvisation was good.

"Tell me, Belle. Tell me, what can I use that will be more sensitive than my fingertips?" he asked as he nipped at her ear, drawing the flesh against his mouth. Making her body turn liquid.

"Your lips?" she offered. His words, and the images they evoked, were almost as erotic as his touch. As his proposed touch.

Her hips arched slightly.

"Ah. Excellent idea." With a gentle kiss to her ear, he lifted and scooted her up the smooth top of the desk. A paper toppled over the side and lightly floated to the carpet. She never saw it end its descent. The moist heat of Wag's breath at her knee had her closing her eyes.

His lips lightly kissed the skin at her thigh. She felt the warm wetness of his tongue in one, too-brief touch.

Every muscle tightened, every atom of her body waited for his next touch.

He dragged his lips upward, along her inner thigh.

"Your skin is perfect. Soft. Maybe I'm not missing anything at all without you wearing panties. Not if I get to do this instead."

Frustration built in her body and she clenched her fists. Yeah, but he was missing the point. He was supposed to be discovering whether she wore panties or not. And he was taking way too long.

When he almost reached the top of her thigh, he switched to her other leg. She groaned her disappointment, arching her body.

Blessed relief swept through her entire body at the light touch of his breath teasing the skin hiding her most secret place. Close. He was so close. Wagner clasped her hips.

"Ah, no panties. That's been driving me crazy all day."

"It was supposed to."

"Now I'm going to drive you crazy."

Then there was no relief at all, only pounding, heady sensation. His tongue swept along the slickness of her body, making her burn.

"Annabelle." His voice sounded torn from his body. "Spread your legs—I want you. I have to be inside you so bad."

GET FREE BOOKS and a FREE GIFT WHEN YOU PLAY THE...

Lucky 7

SLOT MACHINE GAME!

Just scratch off the silver box with a coin. Then check below to see the gifts you get!

YES!

I have scratched off the silver box. Please send me the 2 free Harlequin Temptation® books and gift for which I qualify. I understand I am under no obligation to purchase any books, as explained on the back of this card.

342 HDL D36E   **142 HDL D36U**

FIRST NAME	LAST NAME

ADDRESS

APT.#	CITY

STATE/PROV.	ZIP/POSTAL CODE

7	7	7	Worth TWO FREE BOOKS plus a BONUS Mystery Gift!
🍒	🍒	🍒	Worth TWO FREE BOOKS!
♣	♣	♣	Worth ONE FREE BOOK!
🔔	🔔	🍒	TRY AGAIN!

www.eHarlequin.com

(H-T-12/04)

DETACH AND MAIL CARD TODAY!

The Harlequin Reader Service® — Here's how it works:

Accepting your 2 free books and gift places you under no obligation to buy anything. You may keep the books and gift and return the shipping statement marked "cancel." If you do not cancel, about a month later we'll send you 4 additional books and bill you just $3.80 each in the U.S., or $4.47 each in Canada, plus 25¢ shipping & handling per book and applicable taxes if any.* That's the complete price and — compared to cover prices of $4.50 each in the U.S. and $5.25 each in Canada — it's quite a bargain! You may cancel at any time, but if you choose to continue, every month we'll send you 4 more books, which you may either purchase at the discount price or return to us and cancel your subscription.

*Terms and prices subject to change without notice. Sales tax applicable in N.Y. Canadian residents will be charged applicable provincial taxes and GST. Credit or debit balances in a customer's account(s) may be offset by any other outstanding balance owed by or to the customer.

She moved her legs for him and reached for his big, broad shoulders. "Now. Please." He had her doing a little begging herself.

"One more detail," Wag said, sitting once more. With sure hands, he reached for his middle desk drawer and pulled out a condom.

Annabelle made her eyes wide as she reclined against the desk. "Why, Mr. Achrom, I've never seen *that* in there before."

"I can be spontaneous."

"Pshaw. Spontaneous. I'll show you naughty," she told him, taking the condom from his fingers.

With a light touch, she dragged the wrapper across the heated skin of her chest. Touching the corner to her nipple. Sucking in a breath as it tightened further. Teasing him. And her.

"I just can't let you slip this on." With a quick twist, she tore it apart, throwing the packaging onto the floor. "Hmm," she said as she unrolled their protection slightly. "I know how much you admire precision. With a little effort, I think we can get this on in an interesting way."

She reclined once more against the desk, then dropped the condom at the apex of her cleavage.

His eyes turned to hungry slits and he sucked in a breath. "Ms. Scott, I never realized how many imaginative ideas you have."

"I'm an asset in and outside the office. Now, come here."

Straddling her stomach, Wagner aimed for the condom. The touch of his hot skin between her breasts tormented her. Anticipation singed her nerve endings, making her think of the pleasure yet to come.

Slowly he glided over her, until the rugged tip of him touched the latex of the condom. Wagner groaned as she slowly eased it down his length.

"I'll never look at condoms as a drag again."

A quick, flip reply formed on her lips, but Wagner moved quickly and soon she felt the strong, slick glide of him moving into her body.

Annabelle moaned deep in her throat, tilting her hips higher to meet his thrust.

Wag's hands left her hips and clutched her shoulders, drawing her closer to his chest. She met his force again.

"Anna…Annabelle, don't move against me like that. I—"

A sweeping, growing ache swirled inside her, drawing her body closer to his. She moved against him again. Harder.

Wag groaned, then slid into her again and again. His movements fast, ragged and uneven.

She loved it.

Her climax arced near. She moved against him, wild. Then a blast of erotic sensation squeezed her muscles and she couldn't move anymore…only feel.

Above her, Wag's breathing grew laboured. Under her stroking fingers, his strong back muscles contracted. Lowering her hands, she grabbed the tight hardness of his cute little rear end.

With two more ragged thrusts, Wag filled her.
Better than marshmallows.
Better by a long shot.

6

NO FINESSE. Wagner ground his back teeth. He'd lost all his finesse, pounding into Annabelle like a seventeen-year-old boy just thrilled to have his first chance at bat.

Hell.

Frowning, Wagner disengaged himself from her body, then he tucked her close to his side. He wasn't that selfless. He wanted her near him. Annabelle sighed, a breathy and contented sigh that floated over his skin like a caress as she snuggled closer to his chest.

He could grow hard again with just that one sigh.

She'd done a lot more than sighing moments before. The way she moaned his name as she'd shuddered and writhed beneath him…

His spirits rose. Maybe he hadn't totally blown this. Maybe he'd have another chance to show her he was more than a quick roll on the top of his desk.

Annabelle rubbed her bare leg up and down his shin. Something soft and frilly tickled his hip.

Her skirt. He hadn't even taken off all her clothes. Annoyance lanced his ego. Damn. No finesse.

He drew in the scent of her hair. He loved women's hair. *This* woman's hair, long and curling around his arm, with just a hint of vanilla. His body hardened more. Yeah, just what any woman would want, another tumble on a desk with a man who already proved to be a lousy lay. He had to do something. Fix it.

"How about dinner? Tonight." Good. Out before he could examine any feelings of guilt or pricks of conscience. He should be giving her the easy out.

Annabelle propped herself on her elbow and looked down at him, a smile playing about the red fullness of her lips. Red and full from his kisses.

He still wanted her. Had to be with her more, longer.

"Ah. I never knew that an old-fashioned gentleman coexisted with the crazed sex machine."

"I didn't know, either." Sex machine he could live with. Awesome god of sex would be better. But old-fashioned? Now, no one had ever hurtled an accusation like that at him before. "Nothing in the last twenty-four hours has gone to plan."

"Is that a complaint?" she asked as her hand dipped to stroke his stomach.

"Hell, no."

"Maybe we're both a little more daring than I thought."

"I never knew you were so spontaneous, Ms. Scott. What made you suddenly decide to change?"

An odd look crossed her face and her smile dimmed. Then, with a shake of her head, her smile returned. "I just woke up and things made a lot more sense." Her hand resumed its southerly approach.

His stomach muscles clenched and he caught her hand before it dared any lower. *More than a roll on a desk.* "We'll go to that new Italian restaurant in Bricktown."

Crap. How cheesy could he get? Bricktown had first-date-trying-to-impress written all over it.

"I haven't said yes."

"You will."

An excited gleam lit her eyes and her sexy smile turned eager. "Oh, I do love Bricktown. There's something about the ballpark…"

Annabelle sat up, her breasts moving from side to side. He couldn't look away and it took him a moment to breathe. Had he suggested dinner? What an idiot. He should be ordering in and… "I'll pick you up at seven-thirty."

With a wiggle, Annabelle smoothed her skirt into place. His focus immediately changed from the logistics of setting a mealtime to making a meal of her. What had he been thinking? Why'd he suggest they eat away from this very spot? A quickie on the desk didn't sound so bad, after all. He could work in a few finesse moves.

"I'll meet you there in an hour instead," Annabelle said.

He couldn't understand the feeling of disappointment at losing the opportunity to pick her up like a real date. In fact, from grabbing his tie to shimmying into his office with obviously one goal in mind,

Annabelle had demonstrated loud and clear that this was not about a relationship. It was about sex.

Great, mind-blowing sex.

But still sex. Annabelle was right to define the terms. Picking her up and escorting her home created a whole new set of complications. This was not a date. This was a…hell, he didn't know what it was, but it wasn't good.

"I'll let you wonder what I'm wearing—or not wearing—over dinner."

His disappointment vanished and he drew on his pants. "I never knew you could pull down a zipper with your teeth."

"It's tough, but with the right motivation…" Her words trailed off as she patted the zipper covering his ever-hardening penis.

"Happy to oblige," he said, biting back a groan.

"Oh, and, Wag," she said, smiling, her voice pure seduction, "wear a tie."

ANNABELLE PARKED her car at the Bricktown garage. A quick glance at her dashboard clock confirmed she was early. And a woman must never arrive before a man. Maybe she should try to call Katie again to let her know she was meeting with Wag instead. She'd left a quick message on her friend's voice mail. Belle's shoulders slumped against the seat. That strange, nagging sensation tugged on her again. Ever since Thursday night, whenever Belle thought about Katie, something inside her warned her against picking up the phone. Thursday night…

Her mouth watered and her taste buds craved something sweet. Great, she had time to savor a few marshmallows. Strange. She'd never really craved marshmallows before, but now she wanted them more than chocolate. And that was worrisome. Maybe she should freshen her lipstick instead.

Hmm, or perhaps she'd leave the lipstick off. She'd hate to leave a stain on Wagner's collar... Or maybe she could rub one of her new flavored lip glosses along his rock-hard abdomen and try out a new application technique. *Yeah.*

What taste would he like best? Sinful cinnamon or seductive strawberry?

Five minimarshmallows later, she was good to go. The parking garage was near the ballpark, known to locals as The Brick. She took a few idle steps toward the third-base entrance. The green gates were closed, but the winter pale green of the ballfield compelled her, followed by an even stronger compulsion to run naked through the field. Too, too weird!

With a wrench, she pulled her hands away from the gate. Ordering herself not to look back, she strolled the short distance to the restaurant along the sidewalks stretching on either side of the canal.

She loved this area of the city, where the vibrant purple, yellow and burgundy of the pansies bloomed all winter. Her stomach never failed to wake up at the mouthwatering aroma wafting from the many restaurants—Mexican, Steakhouses, Chinese, Italian—all delectably mixing with the smell of hot dogs, roasted peanuts and popcorn coming from the outdoor vendors' carts.

Today the sun shone brightly and it was warm enough to go without a coat. Many of her fellow Oklahoma City residents were taking advantage of the warmer day to enjoy the beauty of the canal, decorated with light displays, bows and poinsettias.

Winter had never been her favorite season, but now she regarded it with something more than dread. How had she thought of it the night of the party? A promise. A promise of fresh starts.

Like yesterday.

And tonight.

Her body tingled and not all from the thorough loving Wagner had given her on his desk. She could definitely ascribe the tingles to the crotchless panties she'd bought on her way home from work. Each step forward reminded her that soon Wag would discover her latest purchase...and try them out.

Their physical connection was powerful. But what of the emotional one? Her steps slowed. Where had that question come from? Grrr. The old Annabelle butted in everywhere. She didn't want to be practical right now. Those thoughts had never given her Wagner's lips, his frenzied hands, his strong arms holding her close.

She'd loved Wagner for all these long years. Besides Katie, he'd been the only person to ever believe in her. No one, not even her extended family, had stood beside her after her father's scams came to light.

No. She was not going to examine this to death. That's something the old Annabelle would have done. Scrutinize from every angle until every single thrill and tingle of excitement stirring in her soul faded to nothing.

Not anymore. Tonight she'd be free. Free of the guilt and shame of her father, free of worry and responsibility. She'd be the person she could have become if her father hadn't left her with a pile of bills and a family scandal to clean up.

At seventeen the future had lain before her, promising, bright. Annabelle closed her eyes and tilted her cheeks to the sun, letting the warmth heal her battered soul. She couldn't pin down exactly what had changed in her, what had reawakened the spirit she once had, but she wasn't about to question it, either. Tonight, and for as long as she had these wonderful feelings, she'd live and enjoy. Now to find her man.

She discovered him in the crowd gathering by the hostess stand. The sight of him stole her breath away. Okay, a goofball cliché, but those beautiful blue eyes of his, broad shoulders encased in a dark gray suit, gray shirt and gray tie...

Tie. They'd be buying a colorful tie tomorrow.

She took a breath. Her new mantra—wait. She didn't have a new mantra. Just live it and love it. That would work as her new motto. She'd live for these delicious moments to come, and they *would* come, and she'd delight in every one of them.

A bit of lace from her new panties touched an area

her regular old cotton briefs stayed clear of. Belle licked her lips. Wag better eat darn fast. Her body hungered for him.

He sauntered to her side when he spotted her. He didn't greet her with a smile. Instead, an odd tension seemed to surround him. His gaze shifted on her breasts. After four years of his apparent total lack of awareness that she even possessed different body parts than he did, she couldn't resist thrusting her breasts forward a little.

Her nipples tightened under the soft material of her blouse. *That's right, buddy. There won't be any doubt I'm a woman ever again.*

"It will be about ten minutes before a table is ready."

Ah, now she knew what the tension was all about. The old, high-powered raider Wagner Achrom could have any table he wanted. This Wagner…couldn't.

She liked this Wagner better.

Annabelle looped her arm through his, the muscles of his forearm rippling beneath her fingertips. "That's okay. We can walk and enjoy the canal."

After a moment's hesitation, the tension faded from his rugged features and his shoulders relaxed. Wagner stepped along beside her. A bright yellow water taxi, half full of wassail-drinking passengers sailed beside them, the conductor pointing out various sites along the river.

They followed the winding sidewalk in silence, passed by power walkers and a mother pushing a stroller. The unusual warm breeze kissed her face. Brightly wrapped boxes resembling presents circled the tree trunks, filling her with holiday anticipation. A duck family paddled beside them.

"I wish we had some bread," she said.

"Why? Are you that hungry?"

She glanced his way. The corners of his eyes crinkled. Wagner was teasing her. Excitement stole into her heart. She doubted Wagner ever had much teasing in his life. "The bread is only to feed the ducks, silly."

She doubted anyone had ever dared call him silly. For one thing, there'd been no reason to, although she'd spotted glimpses of the man he could have been, had circumstances not made him cut himself off from the softer side of life.

A day, much like this one, flitted across her memories. Feeding the ducks, this time with her father. Her father was a charming blend of irresponsibility and fast talk. A man of ideas and a hunger for money.

A man a lot like Wagner.

He stopped and grabbed her hand, gently pulling her closer to him. "You're really something. Always thinking of others, even ducks, aren't you?"

"They'll be flying south soon. We've fooled them with this late start to winter." The easiness between them waned. She didn't like where her thoughts had headed. She hated the past. Hated how her father had taken money away from the trusting with a smile. That's where the similarities between Wagner and her father ended. Wagner wanted to do something with his ideas. Something more than just make money and fatten the pockets of shareholders.

As of today, she wouldn't think one more thought about her father. She'd ship them off. Gone, sent away like her last loan payment to cover her father's debts.

She lowered her voice to a seductive purr. "Right now I'm only thinking about one thing."

His blue eyes darkened, like a hungry man who'd just discovered a buffet. "Oh, yeah?"

"Oh, yeah," her voice purred, deepened. "Like, right now I'm thinking, 'How long is it before he discovers what I have on under this skirt?'"

Wag smiled and shook his head. "Annabelle? What has gotten into you?"

"You. And you can do it again if you play your cards right. Now feed me. Our ten minutes are up and I've decided I'm hungry after all."

Wagner stopped her from walking away. He drew her into his arms, his gaze locked with hers. He lowered his head and her eyelids drifted shut. His kiss was pure heat and all passion. Annabelle moaned deep in her throat and his hands, stroking her hips, possessively drew her closer.

This was not a passive kiss, but a kiss as equals. Annabelle didn't just sit back and allow herself to be kissed. She kissed back. She gave him as good as he was giving her.

"And to our right, two Oklahoma City residents

are enjoying the canal and all the many options it has to offer," a voice boomed over a loudspeaker.

Wag broke off the kiss at the hoots and applause coming from the water taxi floating alongside them. The captain tipped his hat in mock salute. Stepping to the side, Wagner shielded her body with his.

Ah, here was Wagner trying to be gallant and all she could do was giggle.

"You know, I took a ride on the canal when they did the same thing to another couple. Seemed a lot funnier that time," he said, his voice as dry as Oklahoma in August.

A touch of daring tickled her funny bone. Standing on tiptoe, she wrapped her arms around him, then turned him to face her. Pulling his head lower, she whispered against his lips, "Let's give those sightseers something to tell the folks back home."

She wrapped her arms around his neck and drew him to her tight. His tongue played against her lips and she opened her mouth to him. She returned his kiss with a passion matching his from moments before. Their tongues met and twined.

Cheers echoed from the water taxi, then faded as it glided out of sight. "Think about that during dinner," she said. Then she wiped the remnants of her get-him-every-time red lipstick from his moist lips.

"No problem," he said, the color high along his cheekbones.

She was so hot for Wagner's body, she doubted she'd last through an entire meal without jumping his bones. To her delighted surprise, after the hostess showed them to a table, they settled into relaxed conversation, their banter continuing until their food arrived.

She'd only ever known Wagner as the stiff businessman trying to build his new venture from the ground up. Okay, he was still pretty good being stiff. And a gal could learn to really appreciate stiff in a man. Besides the obvious, she could have all the more fun when her man finally became putty in her hands.

Suddenly, memories of an article she'd read about Wagner in the newspaper a few years back surfaced. Wagner Achrom had a reputation as a major power player and taker. He'd had it all at one time, a recognized name, money and beautiful willing women.

Now he had to wait in line for a table just like the rest of the nine-to-fivers. But the choice had been his and she admired him all the more for turning his back on wealth and power. It was important for her to know why.

"Wagner, I've always wondered about something."

A wicked gleam entered his eyes. "You found out this afternoon."

She smiled and heat settled in her midsection. What do you know? Wag had a sense of humor. "Yes, I know all your secrets but one. Why'd you break off and start your own company?"

The light in his eyes dulled and he reclined against his chair, crossing his arms.

Belle hid a smile. *Nice move, Wag. A corporate trainer*

could write a manual on that body language. But she wasn't going to let him get away with that.

She reached for his hand and squeezed. "I really want to know. You made millions, were very successful. Most people wouldn't give all that up. Couldn't."

A wealth of emotion danced across his face. Then as he regained control, his expression became unreadable.

He wasn't going to tell her. Their easy conversation was over. She'd cut him off from a night of pure fun and ruined their evening. She dropped his hand, reaching for a bread stick, needing something to do.

His lips tightened. "I was ruthless." His voice held an edge she'd never heard before.

"I remember one time the paper called you the King of the Hostile Takeover."

Wagner's lips thinned. "I didn't realize you knew much about my past."

"Pretty hard to avoid the way you make news. The chop shop of the business world."

Wagner laughed, a humorless sound. "Except it was more about stealth than stealing."

"Did you enjoy it?" Her heartbeat quickened. She hadn't realized how important his answer would be to her until this moment.

"Like you said, I made millions."

She lifted an eyebrow. "That's not what I asked."

"Some of the time I enjoyed the ride. It was like a game, thrilling and risky. But the satisfaction was fleeting and for all the wrong reasons. And most of that money was for other people."

"So how did you get into the business, anyway? It was a far cry from realizing your father's ideas and creating new sources of power."

"Same sob stor—I was a kid who grew up poor, picked on. I'm sure you can guess the rest."

"You took on the world to prove something." She liked his no-apologies stance. He didn't dwell on the past. Wagner Achrom was no victim of circumstance. He made his own way in life, made his own rules. "But you said it was for all the wrong reasons."

"I became another rat in the rat race. Happy to screw the next guy as long as my stock stayed high and the shareholders were happy."

"And that's not who you really are."

"Maybe that's *exactly* who I am."

She opened her mouth to protest.

"Don't hold any illusions about me, Annabelle. I don't. This merger, when it happens, when I make it happen, will put me back on top. But this time on my terms."

Wagner Achrom had the most whacked-out sense of self she'd ever met. Yeah, he talked a tough game, but she knew something more dwelled beneath the surface and it wasn't just his need to be back on top.

"Well, what a surprise."

The snide, ugly voice could belong to only one person. Turning in her chair, she let her eyes confirm what her ears told her.

"Not a pleasant one, Rhoads. I thought I saw you skulking about," Wagner said, his voice laced with contempt.

Kenny Rhoads. The man oozed smarm. Born handsome, rich and raised with the belief his family money covered over any problem, the man had grown up without a conscience. The last time she'd seen the man had been at her father's joint trial with him. The one where her father had been sentenced to eight and a half years and Rhoads had walked away a free man.

Arthur Scott had been little more than a con artist, setting up elaborate pyramid schemes. He was slick, but when her father had hooked up with Kenny Rhoads, that's when he'd become ruthless.

Annabelle reached for her water glass and took a sip. It was hard for a daddy's girl to admit jail was where her father belonged. But it was the truth. With Kenny in the cell beside him. But Kenny was a weasel and he'd squeaked off with a fine and a stint of community service.

She eyed him as she returned her glass to the table. "Still stealing from widows and children, Kenny? Kicked any small animals today?" she asked. Okay, she'd never actually seen him harm an animal, but she wouldn't put it past him. But she could verify from experience the man had no qualms about robbing children.

Suddenly a new excitement lifted her spirits. She

felt stronger. A few years ago—heck, a week ago—she would have let this man intimidate her. Not now.

Not with Wagner at her side. The coiled anger emanating from her lover fueled her own inner strength.

His smile widened. "I leave the stealing to the likes of your father."

A low blow. Coming from an even lower man. "Don't forget, I know the truth."

Kenny turned his gaze to include Wagner. "It's almost like a family reunion. I just had a very interesting conversation with a congresswoman by the name of Taggert."

Annabelle tensed. That was the name of the main House member holding up the crucial bill Wagner needed for Anderson to go forward with the merger.

The powerful oil and energy industry was a small community. And since money was to be made there, Kenny Rhoads was bound to appear. All the better if he could cheat someone in the process. Even her father, a consummate con man, had bought Kenny's swindle.

Annabelle watched the interplay between the two men. Wagner was the kind of man Kenny Rhoads despised. And was afraid of. Self-made and successful. Her man never dropped his stare.

Since Wagner wasn't intimidated by him, Kenny turned his attention back to Annabelle.

"How is—"

"Not another word." Wagner stood as he spoke each word. Slowly.

Kenny took a step back. "What?"

"You don't say another word to her."

"Are you threatening me?" Kenny swallowed, able to dole out the anguish and the bullying easily enough, but not able to handle adversity himself.

Wagner must have sensed it, too, because he sat back down.

"Who do you think you are? Why, you're as much a danger to society as her father."

Wagner's cold blue gaze raked Kenny. "I'm dangerous because I have nothing to lose. If you get in my way, I *will* stop you. And I'm to never see you converse with Ms. Scott again. Ever."

Patches of white splotched Kenny's reddening skin. He almost stumbled in his rush to get away from them. The man's discomfiture would almost be laughable if she didn't know the man would use the incident as an excuse to thwart Achrom Enterprises as best he could.

"Why didn't you tell me Kenny Rhoads was involved?" She didn't know whether to be offended or grateful.

Wagner grabbed his drink and drained it. "I didn't know until the meeting."

"But you realized later."

Wagner nodded. He would never lie. Another reason she could trust him. "And what he meant to you, your family."

Annabelle gulped. On some level she'd known Wagner must be aware of her father. Sheesh, everyone in the greater Oklahoma City area must know. The scandal… But he'd never said anything, never judged. It was important he know the truth about her dad.

"About my father—it took me awhile to realize this, but he wasn't some misunderstood man of dreams. He was a crook. He stole from people, and prison…" She swallowed, fighting the lump in her throat again. Discussing her father never rated high on her list. Only Katie knew the basics. "Prison was the best place for him."

Wag didn't say a word. No surprise crossed his face. No disgust changed the way he regarded her— the way it had changed so many in the past.

When he needed her efficient research skills the most, he hadn't asked her to investigate Kenny Rhoads. He'd known what Kenny meant to her and he hadn't told her. Why?

He'd protected her from Kenny's spiteful words tonight in an elemental way. Man to man. Men could be so…delicious. So protective about the things they valued.

Her whole body melted. Oh, Lord, she was growing sappy. And she so didn't want to do that. To become vulnerable. She'd just wanted to keep it light and fun. But the old Annabelle couldn't help poking in her hopeful nose. Did Wagner feel the same way about her? Did he want more than just a fun afternoon?

Annabelle met his gaze, searching for some sign. Dare she hope? Dare she hope Wagner might have fallen for her a little over the years?

Hooded emotion entered those brilliant blue eyes of his. His hand curled tightly around his glass. He straightened his tie. The tie she'd told him to wear. Her fingers itched to tug it.

His cool gaze slid up to meet hers again. "Power and control are the only things that matter to me."

A warning. Loud and clear. He was warning her off. How typical and another clear indication he was anything but a rat only after two things, wealth and influence. Well, three. Hot sex. But she'd let him have that one. Because she'd wanted it, too.

She didn't want to be here anymore. Didn't want to think about Kenny Rhoads or her father or any of the problems of the last few years. No thinking…just feeling.

Pure hot lust for him had her wiggling in the chair. Kicking off her mule, she poked her toes under his pant leg. She traced a lazy path up the sock until she touched his bare skin. Wagner sat straight up in his chair. Delicious.

"Power and control. Oh, the way you said that. It's so hot. So commanding." Her voice lowered, "I want you. *Right now.*"

Disentangling herself from his pant leg, she shoved her foot into her mule and stood.

"Where are you going?" he asked.

"Pay the bill. I'll meet you at the office. If you're lucky, you'll find out what I have on under my skirt."

7

After throwing a few bills onto the table, Wagner reached for her arm. "I'll walk you to your car."

Mmm. No suggestion. A statement. Predatory Wagner was very sexy.

Wagner's hand glided from her elbow to her waist, pulling her closer to his side. She slipped her hand beneath his suit coat, the muscles of his back rippling beneath the soft cotton of his shirt. Her fingertips tingled in response.

He matched his stride to her shorter steps as they strolled along the canal. The setting sun created a postcard-worthy picture of red, green, yellow and lights reflecting off the ripples of the water. The soft, sensual cry of a saxophone drifted from the blues club farther up the canal.

"What level?" he asked.

"Two." Her voice sounded breathless. Urgent anticipation made her want to hurry their ascent up the stairs. But darn if Wagner wasn't taking his sweet, slow time. Many of the cars had left the garage, setting her safe, reliable Volvo in stark relief.

Annabelle didn't want to be safe or reliable. She craved to be dangerous and daring. To be the kind of woman Wagner had finally noticed after all these years.

His warm breath trailed a seductive breeze along her cheek. She traced one finger along the smooth, hard line of his jaw.

Smooth. He must have shaven before joining her for dinner. A lover's thoughtfulness. A shudder of impatient desire shivered through her.

She stared into his eyes. The intense blue of his eyes burned her. She wanted his kiss. Needed to feel him.

His thumb rested provocatively on her bottom lip. Her breathing grew shallow.

She kissed the tip of his thumb and he groaned. With tender strength, he hauled her against his chest and into his arms. His mouth covered hers.

She shared his hunger. Winding her arms around his neck, she sunk her fingertips into the hair above his collar. He crushed her to him. His powerful arms wrapped around her body, drawing her as close as thrillingly possible. Her body flared into a firework. Blazing and smoldering hot. Wagner kissed her hard, his tongue seeking entry into her mouth, while his hands stroked up and down her back.

Her heartbeat quickened and her knees weakened, the force of his desire making her lightheaded. Except she didn't plan to miss a single second of this. Annabelle leaned into his body, her fingers now circling down his back.

His hands moved up her body, stilling at her

breasts. She moaned, deep and low when his thumbs grazed her nipples.

Wagner tore his lips away and rested his forehead against hers. His hands grabbed her forearms, steadying her, then pushed her gently away. His fingers wrapped firmly around her wrists. After several moments, Wagner's hands dropped.

The air in the garage chilled her arms now that he provided no warmth.

Damn.

He'd been thinking again. That was never good.

She'd put a stop to this right now. New Annabelle to the rescue.

Draping herself against her car, she flashed him a smile. A decadent reminder of what had been, a promise of what was to come. She didn't try to hide her arousal. Wagner's eyes followed the line of her leg, along her thigh and stopped at the hem of her clothes.

Ah, yes, buddy. Don't you forget what I have on under this skirt.

Wagner had never backed down from a fight. Never. It was clear he wanted her but was holding back. His groan warned her that not everything was working according to her plan.

"Belle, we have to talk."

Double damn. Ah, yes. Now, *there's* a phrase every lover wanted to hear.

"Did you hear what you called me?" She stood straighter and her heart beat a rapid tempo. "I don't think you've ever called me Belle. How very unprofessional of you, Wagner."

She reached for his tie and tugged at the knot. "Since we're being so unprofessional, maybe we should dispense with this. I see a fire in your eyes."

His long fingers stilled hers. "This was dinner. I didn't expect any—" He stopped and took another breath. "It's been an emotional night. Seeing Rhoads again. You're not acting yourself."

Those words cooled any remaining passion.

Wagner cupped her chin again, drawing her lips to his. She shuddered as he lightly passed his lips across hers. Then he pulled away, kissing the tip of her nose. Her forehead.

"Good night," he whispered.

For a moment their gazes locked. She read promise in his eyes. Some elemental, powerful emotion passed across his face. Her disappointment vanished. "Good night," she echoed.

Turning, she unlocked her car door and Wagner shut it once she buckled her belt. Her fingers trembled slightly as she shoved the key into the ignition. She had to get out of there before she kicked open her car door and demanded he do right by her.

Annabelle chanced one last glance in his direction. He stood by the gray concrete column. His stare never wavered as he watched her drive away from him. With a small wave, she left the garage.

She wouldn't think about it. Reaching for the knob on the radio, she fiddled around until she found a station playing just what she needed to hear—the pounding rhythms of classic rock 'n' roll.

She needed a new plan. Tonight she'd go home and figure out her best one yet.

"Watch your step, Wagner Achrom. You ain't seen nothin' yet."

STAY AWAY from the nice ones, Wagner warned himself.

Stay away from the nice ones. And with Annabelle, he should add an expletive. Stay the *hell* away. The seductive curve of her hips, the rounded flare inviting a man's touch, *his* touch, that alone warranted a caution sign.

He swallowed his regret as he fished out his car keys. But Annabelle was one of the nice ones. Or had been until a few days ago. Until she caught the seduction flu. And gave it to him yesterday. Now she was naughty.

And nice.

Damn. Stay away from the nice ones. Time to back off. He'd already let Annabelle down by surrendering to passion this afternoon in his office. Making love to her violated the ideals of trust and respect his parents had preached to him.

And if Wagner followed through on what his body wanted once he and Annabelle were alone, he'd let her down even more.

Wagner slammed his car door with gusto. He knew the score. No strings, no expectations, no regrets. He'd always tried to date only women who understood and wanted the same kind of relationship. And even if a nice girl said she understood the routine, you still stayed away from them. Because deep down, they might harbor some hope. And they might just transfer some of that hope to him. Then it would be his mom and dad all over again.

He'd seen what his dad's job losses had done to his mother. The financial insecurity, the shift work, not to mention dealing with the mood swings and bitterness of a man whose dreams slowly died over the years, had beaten his mom, too. He watched his mother's love for her husband slowly flare out, until only her sense of duty and obligation kept her in the marriage.

Wagner's future didn't offer much more than that. He'd rather walk away right now than subject Annabelle to that kind of life and end up disappointing her.

His assistant didn't need any more baggage. She'd already pulled herself up from one near-hopeless situation. There was no way he would cause the lights in Annabelle's eyes to dim the way they had in his mother's.

What *had* Annabelle worn under her skirt? His body still burned at the spot where her hot breath teased the skin behind his ear as she'd whispered her taunt.

And here he stood, just as eager as he had been two hours ago. Harder than a seventeen-year-old boy on prom night. He had to have her again.

Shifting into first, he snaked his car around the concrete pillars of the parking garage. He should be trying to salvage what he could from his disastrous meeting with Smith and Dean. Figuring out a way to destroy Rhoads. For his sake and for Annabelle's.

He should be driving to his office to verify with his Washington contact when the House bill would be coming out of committee.

He was on his way to the office, all right, and not at the safest of speeds in his condition, not to work, but to avoid making love to a woman he'd sworn to shield from himself not forty-eight hours ago. Four years of fighting to be something…someone different and he'd landed right back in the exact same place. Shit, he was losing his mind.

Wagner looked in the rearview mirror as he changed lanes. The face he'd glimpsed was familiar in a way he didn't want to remember or acknowledge. His father. He resembled him. Great, another not-so-pleasant realization.

The blue eyes staring back looked nearly identical to his old man's. Letting down a woman who trusted him was standard operating procedure for dear old dad. Although he doubted Pop had sunk so low as to desk-boink the one woman who held a modicum of respect for him.

Unfortunately, he couldn't wait to do it again.

And again.

Annabelle should be out of his system.

But after yesterday and spending the evening with her—her laughter, her conversation, her spirit—he just wanted her more than ever.

He had to know what she wore under that skirt. Maybe he could call her and ask. What an idiot. Twinkling Christmas lights sped past his window as he navigated his car toward his office. Thong, the lacy things women thought men liked, hell, he didn't care, he'd pull them down with his teeth. If she wore nothing, and he hoped to heaven that was the case, he'd…

No. No. No.

No teeth, no kisses, no touching. Period. It was explanation time. Break-off time. Of course, Annabelle would have to stay at least ten feet away during the conversation. In the outer office. Wearing an overcoat.

He'd carefully explain why getting involved with him was such a bad idea. He'd suggest they both forget about the incident. And everything would be normal again. He'd get his merger, his cash and his sanity back. All in one nice neat conversation.

An excellent plan.

He'd explain all of that to her in the morning. Behind his desk.

THE RED LIGHT on the answering machine was blinking faster than her last boyfriend could suggest, "Let's go dutch." The tiny bulb would burst if she didn't put the machine out of its flashing misery. Who could be calling her so many times? Nervous tension shoved aside some of the wonderful sexual glow Wagner had left her in. She depressed the button with one newly manicured red-tipped nail.

"Annabelle, it's Katie. It's extremely import—"

Skip.

"If you're there, pick up the phone. It's Katie, call me, I have to tell you some—"

Skip.

"Where are you? I called you at wor—"

Skip.

"Call me no—"

Katie Sloan. Her best, most trusted and dearest friend in the world. The woman Annabelle shared everything with and counted on more than anyone.

But everything inside her screamed to stay away from Katie. She didn't know why. Wasn't sure she wanted to know why. She trusted her instincts, however.

And there were still five messages left to be heard. Caller ID was invented for times like these. She flipped through the name and time stamps. Nope. All the other messages appeared to be from Katie, as well. Turning off her ringer, Annabelle headed to the bathroom.

A long, luxurious soak in a bathtub full of bubbles was just what she needed. Making love on Wagner's desk might be great for the body, but it was hell on the back. Plus, her tummy was still a little sore from all the sit-ups she'd done the night before. Which reminded her…

Fifty sit-ups later, she sank into the foamy bubbles with a sigh. In the past, she'd tried Pilates, yoga, even cardio kickboxing, but who knew the mythic exercise-induced endorphins would come from a sit-up?

She actually enjoyed doing them. Looked forward to doing more.

Not unlike Wagner. Boy, if Katie knew what she'd done with Wagner, she'd flip. Just the thought of Wagner made her heart race.

Annabelle really wanted to phone Katie, to tell her all about it, but something was holding her back. Katie had never been a downer before. If anyone was the realist in their friendship, she was. So, why the trepidation now?

Because Katie has something to say you don't want to hear.

Where did that outrageous and truly irritating thought come from? Sounded like something she'd say a few days ago. Something before the party and her epiphany not to take her job so seriously….

She sank back against the back of the tub, the bubbles floating higher. Heck, she wasn't going to think about it. Any of it. She had a new job to find and a man to seduce. A delicious tingle fluttered between her legs. Not that he'd been all that hard to seduce.

Except tomorrow.

Wagner really needed to work, followed by a scintillating evening watching C-SPAN. The bill was scheduled to go to a vote tomorrow night. Hm. New plan. Make C-SPAN sexy.

ANNABELLE SCOTT WANTED his body. And only that. He didn't like that at all.

Okay, he liked it a little.

Hell, he didn't know how he felt. He should be ecstatic. What man wouldn't be? A woman, a beautiful sexy woman, one he'd apparently been lusting after for the past four years, finally took matters into her own hands. And him. Damn.

He grew hard at just the thought of her hands on his body. And he'd already had her once today. The specter of the seventeen-year-old boy reared his head again.

Although, in this case, his eagerness could have some advantages. Multiple advantages. Wonderful, pleasurable advantages.

Keep your mind on business.

Wagner hiked up the wooden stairs to his garage apartment. He unlocked the door and shut it with his foot, balancing his briefcase and an armload of files. Switching on the overhead light with his elbow, he didn't bother glancing at the empty space on the left wall.

His last good painting. Sold for quick cash a week ago.

He flipped the light off again, despising the way the brightness made the bare walls look even starker.

That painting had been his first purchase. The first real item of value he'd bought after making that initial crucial deal. The one that got him noticed, put his name on the map.

A map long since burned to ash.

But soon to be reborn.

The endgame was near. Still, dozens of details still

needed to be battled out and his assistant wasn't making it any easier for him to concentrate.

And making love to her only had made it worse. Now that he knew what fire and passion they shared, all he could think about was doing it again. And again.

Keep your mind on business.

Stalking to his drafting table, he picked up the schematic for his solar-fuel-cell relay. He scanned his design searching for mistakes, errors, one more time. He found none. This was it. He knew it. The design was true. Cheap power from a free source. This was what he was meant to do. Not buy companies and strip them for parts. What had Annabelle called him? The chop shop of the business world.

Wagner smiled at her assessment, then groaned as he grew hard again. All his carefully outlined plans shattered around her. Annabelle was a priceless variable.

Think about the schematic, he told himself. It was at least easier to deal with than Annabelle. He remembered seeing his father slumped over the drawing table in this same way, fiddling with one design or another.

Was he just like his father?

He yanked the pull string of the green glass and brass banker's lamp. The lamp had been his father's. Wagner's few memories were of his dad tinkering in the basement until all hours of the night, shrouded by the light this very lamp provided. It was kind of a sick twist that the lamp was now illuminating his own plans. Or perhaps failures.

Wagner fiddled with the beaded lamp pull.

He hated the way his father had rushed through dinner, if even that, to climb down the steps to the basement and work on his "next big deal." Time for throwing around a ball, fishing or whatever it was sons were supposed to do with their fathers never arose. Hell, he didn't know.

The only good memories he had of his father were the few, but treasured, invitations to his inventor's basement. After turning on the lamp, his dad would unroll the drawings and blueprints and point out something that was going to make their family rich.

That first invitation…how old had he been then? Six? Seven?

They'd shared the excitement that night together. The way he'd imagined other dads behaved with their sons. He'd longed for the closeness.

His father had been a man of incredible highs and depressing lows. When things were good, his mom had smiled and his dad would twirl her around the kitchen, dancing to silent music.

"This is it, baby. The one we've been waiting for. Enjoy that casserole, son. Won't be eating that much longer. Steak from now on. Steak and lobster."

His mother would laugh and he'd dream of a bicycle. The kind Jacob Croger rode.

And then the bottom would fall out. His patent would fail, his hesitant backers would bail. There'd be no dancing in the kitchen. His mother would have to get a job at night. After tucking him in bed, she'd leave to stock grocery-store shelves or count out newspapers for early delivery.

Their house would be dark and his mother would talk quietly, hushing him when he came home from school.

Then his father would hit upon a new idea. The pattern followed itself time and time again. Only, the highs would come less often and the downs were always lower than the time before.

His mother always had smiled and supported her husband. Until one day the low had nearly killed her spirit. His father's growing frustration had only added to the already mounting tension in the household. Little money, a husband and father who on his best days could be described as distant and moody.

His father had died chasing the elusive dream of wealth and power. Wagner once had it in his grasp. Steak-and-lobster days.

And he almost had it once more.

Life for his mother had been tough. Counting his dad, she had two children to take care of, acting as mother, father and breadwinner.

He'd never saddle a woman with those kinds of problems. Yeah, he was more and more like his father. He'd already drawn Annabelle into that kind of cycle. What was that emotion slamming into him for the last two days? Guilt.

Fortunes could be made. But lost just as easily.

And he'd involved Annabelle, the same way his father had involved his family.

Disgust filled him. After shoving away from his drawing table, he headed for the kitchen sink and splashed some water onto his face. Crap. Forget not being able to look at himself in the mirror—Wagner didn't want to chance catching his reflection on the chrome water faucet.

The last thing he wanted Annabelle to know was how desperately he needed this merger to come through. How he couldn't offer anything to a woman right now.

Hey, hold up. When had he started thinking about offering her something more? Annabelle appeared to only want, well, his body.

He was the luckiest man on earth. Why did he feel so empty?

Control.

He'd learned a long time ago to control that emptiness. To control every weakness, beat back any inconsistency and stay focused on the goal. It was how he'd supported his mother, put himself through school and climbed his way to the top.

Tight-fisted control had eluded him since Monday, when Annabelle sauntered in wearing pink and a dare on her lips.

Wagner yanked the lamp pull, plunging the room into darkness.

Control. Now to reclaim it.

8

SOMEONE WAS KNOCKING at the door.

Scratch that, someone was pounding on the door. Grrr. She'd finally gotten to the good part in her book. She sank lower into the bubbles of her bath. Of course, the scene in the book couldn't compare to the good part in Wagner's office.

The pounding intensified. This time she growled out loud as she slammed the bookmark in place. Warm water sloshed over the sides of the tub as she rose and wrapped a loose towel around her body.

It had to be Katie. A mixture of irritation and guilt had Annabelle tugging the towel tighter around her breasts. Okay, if she were honest, she had been avoiding her best friend. But really, it was after midnight. She padded quickly on the carpet to her front door.

Rising on tiptoe, she peered through the peephole. A very worn-and-tired-looking Wagner leaned against the door frame. A Wagner without a tie.

Yummy.

Heart pounding, she turned the dead bolt and

opened the door. Who cared about bubbles when a man couldn't stay away? "Changed your mind?"

Wag raked a rapidly heating gaze up and down her towel-draped body. Water pooled at her feet and the cool night air hardened her nipples against the terry cloth.

A flush formed along his cheekbones. But he also looked determined. "This isn't why I came over."

She let the towel slip. "It's not?"

Wag's gaze followed the path of the towel, then quickly shifted upward again. He reached to straighten a tie that wasn't there. "Dammit, woman, give me a little more credit than that."

"Then why are you here?"

The lights from a passing car drew Wagner's attention for a moment, then he leaned toward her. The scent of him sent her nerves tingling all over again. "Invite me in, Annabelle. I don't want to say this on your front porch."

She opened the door wide and swept her hand toward the couch. "Forgive me for being such a poor hostess. Can I offer you…anything?"

The muscles along his jaw tightened. "This is ending."

His clipped words rang harsh. And false.

"Why?" Hmm.

He looked her dead in the eye. "It's not fair to you. I won't—" He looked around the room. At the clock above the mantel. At her laptop on the couch.

At the bag of marshmallows on the coffee table. Looking everywhere.

But not at her.

Finally his gaze met hers, his face grim. "There was a time in my life when engaging in sex for sex's sake was par for the course. It's not something I'm proud of today. The thing is, that was a different time in my life, when—"

"Money, sex and power were yours for the taking?"

"That's right. And although my circumstances are changed, one thing hasn't. I'm not aiming for any kind of commitment. I do things solo."

Ah. Now it was clear. Wagner was warning her off. Again. Just one more example of his honor. One more reason why Wagner Achrom was so easy to love. "Look, Wagner, you seem to be under a misconception here. I don't want a relationship."

"You don't?"

She shook her head emphatically. "No." Liar. *Big* liar.

"Why not?"

Annabelle wanted to laugh, he almost sounded offended, but she was done talking.

"I thought I'd made it clear I wasn't interested in anything other than a little sex. Don't you trust me?" *Crap.* Where had that hurt tone come from?

Things had changed since that confrontation in the restaurant. She hadn't realized it until just this moment, hearing the ache in her own voice. That oh, so tender kiss at her car. His actions demonstrated how deep and raw his emotions were.

Wagner grabbed her shoulders, pulling her to him. "No. Dammit, because I don't trust myself."

Annabelle stood in his embrace and simply breathed in Wagner. Allowed the heat of him to seep into her chilled flesh. For a moment, she felt like her old self again. Vulnerable and in love with her boss.

Wagner didn't trust himself. Didn't trust himself with her. That was good. Right? Her breath hitched. It was confirmation that she meant more to him that just a good time now. She held on to his words a moment longer.

Wagner wanted to end it. A hint of doubt crept into her mind. Maybe this wasn't the right time for sexual interludes. Maybe she should just accept his words. Set him free and he'd come back when…

Sexually daring.

What the hell was she thinking? No. Until a few days ago, Wagner hadn't noticed her. She would not go back. Couldn't. She'd win this battle.

But she'd do it by bringing the war to him.

Taking a step back, she met his wary gaze and clicked her tongue. "Oh, well, that makes this all very simple. You don't have to trust yourself. You just have to trust me. Don't think. Act."

Annabelle dropped the towel.

Wagner stood before her, swallowing. He whacked the door shut with his foot, his gaze never straying from hers.

She stood before him for a moment, then turned. "The bedroom's this way." Taking a few steps, she paused only to look over her shoulder. "I dare you."

With a growl, Wagner caught her in his arms and threw her over his shoulder fireman style. Laughing, she reached over and grabbed his sexy rear end in both hands. Once in her bedroom, he tossed her onto her recently purchased ruffly purple-and-green comforter.

"What am I going to do with you?" he asked roughly against her neck.

"I could give you some suggestions," she teased.

Rolling to her back, she reclined against the pillows. Wagner kicked off his shoes and tore the shirt off his chest. It was the sexiest damn thing she'd ever seen. A man, pushed to the brink of his control, giving in. No, not to the brink. Predatory challenge laced the blueness of his eyes. Wagner was ordered strength as he grasped his belt. A moment later, his pants dropped to the floor. He stalked over to the bed.

He hauled her to his chest, then turned her until her back was to him. The heat of his erection pressed against the small of her back.

His lips found the sensitive area below her ear. "*I'm* daring." His whispered words sent a shiver racing down her neck and along her body. She'd finally unleashed the controlled animal in him. The barely controlled.

She pressed against him, but he set the pace of their lovemaking. His hands didn't linger, didn't tease, but dared. One hand found the taut tip of her breast, while his other nestled between her legs. She cried out as he slid a finger down the slick heat of her body.

"You're mine now, Belle. Mine. Say it." The words ripped from his chest.

"I'm yours." Her body shook, already close to the point of climax.

"Where's the protection?"

She swallowed, hardly able to speak. "Top drawer of the nightstand."

With a nip to her neck, Wagner backed away.

"What the hell is this?"

Annabelle turned, mortification dampening her ardor. He'd found the Blue Boa.

"It was a gag gift. From Katie."

He opened the box lid and pulled out the massive blue vibrator. With a flick of a finger, Wag fired Blue to pulsating life.

"I've never even used the thing," she told him over Blue's loud hum.

A gleam entered his eyes.

"I was too embarrassed to throw it away. With my luck, that would be the day my trash bag fell open."

"Hmm." It was obvious he didn't believe her.

"Don't men give gag gifts?" Okay, she would not become defensive over a household appliance. It was just as useful as a toaster or a washing machine.

"Not ones like this." Wagner flipped another switch and Blue began to throb and thrust between them.

Despite the small twinge of embarrassment, she

was intrigued. "Better watch your step. You could be replaced by modern technology."

His gaze met hers, a rugged smile pulled at his lips. "I'm not intimidated."

"Oh." A jolt of new desire coursed through her body. Did he mean to...?

He turned Blue off and dropped the toy on the bed next to his muscled thigh. After retrieving a condom, he grasped her shoulders. "Where were we?"

With quick movements, he rolled Annabelle over onto her side until once more he lay flattened against her back.

"Loop your top leg behind mine," he commanded. His hushed words sent another flood of desire between her legs. Wagner licked a sigh-inducing circle below her ear as she complied.

He stroked her clitoris, dipping into her slickness. Heady sensations centered where he touched and she thrust her hips against his. His tight groan was like a caress. Just as arousing.

"You're ready for me," he said. Not really a question.

Then he glided into her. Filling her completely with a thrust. His fingers found her clitoris, circling and teasing.

War waged in her. A battle between the unbelievable need to thrust against his hand or against the throbbing of his erection. Frustration drove her wild.

Annabelle cried out when his fingers left her skin. Then her nerve endings fired up in anticipation as the hum of Blue surrounded her.

Without preamble, Wagner lightly stroked Blue's buzzing side along the most sensitive part of her. She bucked at the touch, his penis inching deeper.

"That feels so good." Her words were a moan as she neared orgasm. She clenched and sought contact, battling, fighting for more.

Wagner nibbled her ear. "Not yet," he whispered and pulled Blue away.

Gasping, Annabelle sagged against his chest, her back slick. The sound of her harsh breathing echoed through her bedroom. Wagner moved within her, long, slow strokes. In complete control. Unlike her. She was wild.

He traced the curve of her ear with his tongue. "More?" he growled.

She nodded. A rocket of sensation shot through her body as Wagner stroked her with Blue while thrusting deeply inside her. Annabelle could no longer meet his strokes, but simply thrashed in his embrace as he drove her wild.

Wagner tantalized her once more time by removing Blue, then returning to her hungry body.

"Now," Wagner groaned near her ear, his voice tinged with yielding power.

Then—

Nothing.

Blue spun a few weak circles, then nothing.

Gut-wrenching disappointment ripped at nerves, her body quaked for fulfillment.

"Dammit," Wagner said as he tossed Blue aside.

His fingers, hard and tender, found the spot Blue had so deliciously tormented. Infinitely better.

A rising crest of emotions and sensations pummeled her. Wagner drove into her, escalating her pleasure.

"Belle." Her name was an agonized roar laced with satisfaction.

She fell asleep in his arms.

But she woke up alone.

GOOD INTENTIONS couldn't fight a slipping towel.

Wagner locked his car and dragged his sorry self up the stairs to his apartment. The wind kicked up, slamming cold air into his back.

Good. He deserved it.

He couldn't fight himself while holding a sleeping Annabelle in his arms. Making love to her—hell, just breathing air in the same room as her made him forget all the reasons why.

And they were good reasons. All of them.

He just couldn't remember a damn one of them right now.

ANNABELLE DOUBLE-CHECKED the address she had on file for Wagner. Strange, she'd never visited him before at his home. And the garage apartment perched in front of her didn't fit with her image of him. Rickety wooden stairs, chipped yellowing paint on the door, flaking from the windows.

Frowning she glanced at the piece of notebook

paper again. Two choices sprang to mind. Either ascend the stairs and knock or fire up the engine, do a three-point turn and go back to her apartment. And ignore Katie's telephone calls some more. She shifted in the front seat of her car.

And then there was the chance she could drive Wagner wild all over again. Or have him drive her wild. She'd never be the same after last night. Okay, that actually made three choices. Of course, number three depended on number one, so maybe number three really wasn't a selection, more of a side benefit.

Mind rambling. The first stage of nervousness. Gosh, she was actually a little bit apprehensive. Odd, she hadn't been nervous since she decided to seduce Wagner in the first place—her reason for being here today.

Choice one. Definitely. *Make C-SPAN sexy*. Oh, yeah.

No real decision needed to be made. Besides, when had she ever managed to maneuver a nice three-point turn? Grabbing her new hot 'n' handy purse, the latest fashion for the bad girl on the go, she quickly opened her car door. The stairs weren't as rickety as she assumed and, if Wagner waited at the top, she could topple them two at a time. In heels. Ah, the joy of accessories.

She waited several long minutes for him to answer, her foot beginning a tapping cadence on the landing. She'd better stop that. She'd hate to dislodge any nails holding these stairs together. At the top, looking down, her misgivings about the solidness of the structure returned. Finally the door opened to reveal a very wet and wicked-looking Wagner.

It served him right after getting her out of her bathtub.

Okay, it wasn't the "towel wrapped low on the hips" fantasy. Or even the "hastily donned boxers" daydream. But she'd argue the "button-fly jeans, minus one button properly fastened, and nothing else" fantasy beat those others hands down.

And the towel. That towel draped loosely around his neck, catching the water from his wet hair. The citrusy smell of his soap drifted toward her.

She quelled the urge to suck in a deep breath. "Guess I caught you in the shower."

A water droplet cascaded from a lock of dark hair at his temple. Annabelle watched as it rolled down his freshly shaven cheek and splashed above the tanned skin over his collarbone.

The beginnings of an erotic smile tugged at his lips. She ached to lick away the moisture. Instead, she followed the slow, rounding, tortuous path the water droplet took over the muscles of his chest, down the tight, better-than-a-six-pack abs and lower.

Should she grab the two ends of the towel and pull his lips toward hers?

Maybe help the other buttons release their package? Nah. She'd been making things a little too easy for Wagner Achrom.

"I gave you the day off," he said, rubbing the towel through his dark wet locks.

"I know, but I couldn't let you play hooky from work. You have to share all the fun of watching exciting government debates and votes. I'm part of this, too, you know. Until I quit, we're a team."

In more ways than one, buddy.

"Don't look suspicious. I have nothing up my sleeve. Or my skirt, for that matter. If you want, I'll even prove to you my panties aren't crotchless."

"What?"

"My little surprise from yesterday, crotchless panties."

Now that smile of his turned full-blown sexy. With a wink, she slipped past him and entered his apartment.

And stopped.

If anything, the inside of his home appeared worse than the dilapidated outside. The room contained nothing more than a beat-up futon, in worse shape than something a poor college student would throw away, a TV on a plastic dairy crate and a drawing table. Now she understood why he'd said he didn't want to go to his place. His place was sorely lacking…in just about everything.

And by that awkward stance and defensive body language he exuded at the moment, he didn't like her seeing how he lived. Although she'd never witnessed it personally, there was the ruthless Wagner and she was very familiar with the professional Wagner, the controlled Wagner and lately the passionate Wagner. But never had she been privy to the uneasy Wagner.

"You know, for a person who doesn't have any furniture, you're awfully particular about where you sit. Not on the desk. Not on the couch," she said, injecting mock-tired exasperation into her voice.

"You didn't hear me complaining."

She smiled. "You're right. I didn't."

Tension stretched between them. Unlike the sexual battle tugging between them the last two days, this tug-of-war held an emotional zing. Oh, they'd danced around the quandary quite nicely. She'd side-stepped the issue herself after his dinner invitation by dropping her towel the night he came over to end it. But now she'd invaded his home. And now their circumstances were different. She'd made it different.

"I'm here to watch C-SPAN with you. And to celebrate."

He lifted an eyebrow, a dubious expression if she ever saw one.

"Where's the champagne?" he asked.

She held up a foam cup from Sonic. "I celebrate with diet cherry colas." A knock sounded at the door. "And pizza delivery."

Ten minutes later, they sat shoulder to shoulder on his futon, flipping through the channels until they found the House vote.

"I never thought I'd order a pizza and toast C-SPAN with a diet drink," Wagner said, taking a swig through the red straw.

"Your usual celebrations more of the champagne variety?"

"Somehow I like this much better."

The Speaker of the House pounded his gavel. The formal proceedings would begin in moments.

"This could take hours."

Mmm. Hours. "I think we can occupy our time," she said and she nibbled a bite of his pizza.

A slat from the futon poked into her back and she shifted.

"I don't normally sit on that side," he told her.

Even as broke as she was after her father's embezzlement four years ago, she still managed to sit on something comfortable.

Her stomach pitched. Confusion and a little bit of dread charged into her mind. Something wasn't right. Something she obviously hadn't wanted to face until now. Wagner paid her an extraordinary salary. One she'd used to pay off most of the debts her father had left her. But she had to know the truth.

"Wagner, are you completely broke? As in nothing left, everything gone?" For a moment, all she heard was the blood rushing in her ears.

He hesitated, then reached to his neck. As if to adjust his tie? "Dinner on the canal was the last of the petty cash. I'm officially living on the edge."

Annabelle surged to her feet. What had he said about fortunes being lost? Anger, fear and awe almost left her speechless. Almost. "But you had no money. You could have gotten rid of me a long time ago. Should have."

Wagner raised an eyebrow. "I knew about your situation. The bills, you wanting to go to school. You had a dream. I took a gamble. It paid off. More than I ever expected."

A wave of emotion, so conflicting and overwhelming, engulfed her. Those debts were a shameful burden. How could he be so blasé about something she thought she'd hidden so well?

She should have been embarrassed, but instead she wanted him more than ever.

This time though for a different reason. She'd thought she loved him before. But those feelings barely resembled the emotion, the ache she felt for him now. Then it had been admiration and chemistry. Now it was his honor, his laughter, his soul.

"I, uh, don't know what to say." She reached for her hair, twisting it around her index finger. Darn. She hadn't twisted her hair in days. The return of a bad habit.

"That's funny, for the last week you've seemed to have all the answers."

"Now I don't have any at all. Just questions."

The smile on Wagner's face faded. "Don't look to me for the answers." He lifted a curl off her shoulder and brought the strands to his nose. "You make me hunger. The scent of you. I tried to fight this. This wanting you to the point of career suicide."

"And now?"

He traced the line of her lower lip with his finger, drawing sparks of desire at the lightest touch. Oh, and his gaze…his gaze pulled her in. He gazed at her as if she was unique and special.

"Now I want to kiss you." His fingers clasped her chin, drawing her lips to his. When she expected the touch of his mouth, she felt the shocking surprise of his tongue. He traced the outline of her lips, the seam of her mouth. Not seeking entrance, just tasting her. Only exploring.

Annabelle burned in the wake of his tongue, on fire for the touch of his lips. Whimpering in the back of her throat, she urged him on. If she didn't have a real kiss soon she'd explode.

Then finally the velvet softness of his lips, followed by the hard demand of his mouth devouring hers. An incredible kiss.

She hadn't even known she desired, yearned for this branding kiss. Pulsing life and vibrant need pounded in every pore of her skin and in every atom of her being.

The man could do things with his lips.

Belle reached up, twined her arms behind his neck and met his gaze. Heavy-lidded, his pupils dilated. His breathing harsh. Their kiss had affected him as much as her.

"Keep your eyes open," he commanded. "I want to see the passion flare in your eyes as I make love to you."

An aching shudder passed through her body. Oh, yes, she wanted that, too. She nodded.

An eternity stretched before he touched her. Her

fingers growing restless to touch him again, she began to play with his hair. She was impatient yet wanted these moments to last. She wanted Wagner with everything she had to give.

But it was a dangerous giving.

For one moment, a self-protective hesitation flooded her instincts. Everything would be different after they made love this time. No games, no daring. Real. Real emotion. Real heartache.

She couldn't drag her eyes away from his face. Wagner was beautiful, really beautiful with his strong jaw, high cheekbones. She even found the bump on his nose sexy as hell. Now the harsh planes and lines were softened with tender strength. His intense gaze was aimed only at her.

All her hesitation fled. This was *it*. She knew that now.

The heat of his body, the pent-up tension in his muscles, he wanted her more than mergers, business deals and making it back to the top. Yet he remained still, a contained bundle of sexual energy.

Then she knew.

He was holding back to allow her to make the final decision. Because this time would be different. They both knew that as truth, sensed it. Today…making love now would change everything. Because now it would be more than just hot sex, it really would be *making love*.

And she didn't care. Only he mattered. Only this moment.

"Make love to me, Wagner."

He didn't need another syllable of encouragement. With a growl, he scooped her up into the strength of his arms and carried her down the hall and to his bedroom.

The room held no ornamentation, just a mattress and box springs in the middle of the barren space. But the woven comforter was a ravishment fantasy come to life. The rich burgundy jacquard stripes invited her to slide her hand down the fabric. She couldn't wait to roll around on it. Roll around on it with Wagner.

What kind of decadence lay underneath?

The comforter must have been left over from his wealthier days. One of the few things he apparently had left. Guilt pounded at her heart. He'd sacrificed for her.

Wagner released her legs and she slid down to the floor. Kicking off her shoes she hopped onto the bed. Wagner seized her arms and pulled Annabelle to him, molding her curves to the tight lines of his body.

No hesitation lingered in this embrace, no waiting. His mouth landed on hers with a familiar intensity and Annabelle relished his urgency.

"You taste like heaven," he told her, his lips trailing down the sensitive skin of her throat. Annabelle grasped his head, tangling her fingers in his hair, holding him to her body.

"I'm taking off your clothes. Slowly," he said. His fingers seized the hem of her woolen sweater.

Yes, she wanted that, too.

His hands brushed the sensitive skin under her breasts and he pulled the material higher. Lifting her arms, he yanked the sweater over her head and tossed it onto the floor. The shock of cool air on her skin, then the warmth of Wagner's hands on her back, had her nipples cresting, aching. Her jeans soon joined her pullover.

She lay before him in just her bra and panties, open and exposed in a way she'd never been before in their love play. Because this time was not just playing at being naughty. This time was real.

Wagner traced the curving, lacy line of her bra, following the rise and fall of her breasts. Her nipples tightened further, aching for his more intimate touch.

Annabelle wanted them under the comforter and his hand on her body. Now.

Scrambling, she pushed the heavy fabric down, the comforter falling to the floor.

Silk. Champagne silk sheets.

Cool and smooth against her skin, she reclined against the soft, overstuffed pillows.

Wagner stood, finally unbuttoning his jeans. Then he stretched his long length beside her, touching from shoulder to hip to thigh. Wagner's skin was warm and hair-roughened. She wanted to touch him. She reached up and traced the patterns of hair on his chest.

But he grasped her hand, stopping its exploration. "Later." His voice held delicious promise.

After pushing her hands to her sides, he glided his

fingertips in a slow lazy path from her hips, over her waist, past her rib cage and cupped her breast, molding and shaping her aching flesh until he lowered his lips and brought her nipple into his mouth.

Annabelle exhaled slowly. It felt so good. He felt so good.

"You like this, Belle. Tell me," he urged.

"Yes," she whispered, closing her eyes.

"Nope. Remember our agreement. No closing your eyes."

With struggling resolve, she lifted her lids. Wagner's gaze met hers, the blue depths stormy once more.

"I want to see your eyes when I do this."

His fingers slipped beneath the elastic of her panties, finding her most sensitive area. A light touch, an almost not-there touch. But it brought a fire to her body. Annabelle felt wild and primitive.

"Wagner," she gasped as his touch became even more intimate. "Now, Wagner. Now," she said as she reached for him.

"Slowly," he said, grabbing hold of her fingers. His mouth lowered to hers in a kiss that branded. "I'm going to drive you crazy with my mouth. And my lips."

Then he moved down her body, his fingers pushing her panties to the floor. He kissed her, making her pant. With one, slow lick, wave after crashing wave hit her body.

Then he did it again.

When the tidal wave of her orgasm ebbed, he whispered in her ear. "Look at me," he commanded tenderly.

Annabelle's lids fluttered open and she met his piercing blue gaze.

"You closed your eyes," he said.

How was she supposed to follow his rule during *that*?

"I want to see your eyes when I enter your body."

The blue of his eyes darkened to a deep indigo. His gaze never left hers. His fingers gently stroked the unbelievable heat growing between her legs. Annabelle sucked in a breath as she felt the probing of his erection.

The sensation of him sliding into her almost overwhelmed her. Heat and power. Annabelle arched her back to meet the single thrust that would fully join them. Nestled fully inside her, he cupped her chin, drawing her gaze to meet his.

Wagner drove into her slowly.

Annabelle cupped him. Wanting more. Wanting fast. Wanting hard. Lifting her hips, she met him in a hard thrust.

He groaned above her. "Anna—Annabelle, don't do that. I won't last if you do that."

Thrilling. It was thrilling to make this big strong man live for her body. Her body's need for him.

She lifted to meet him again, her body so near to climax every atom attuned to him and the sensations surrounding his hot, hard length. Lifting her legs, she hooked her ankles behind his back.

A sound, ripped from his chest, signaled the change in him. He drove into her, harder and faster.

"Wagner, yes."

Then she fell over the edge, nothing more than spinning sensation. He pumped into her one last time and his warmth flooded her.

Nothing would ever feel as good as this. Nothing. Then she couldn't keep her eyes open any longer.

WAGNER LOOKED at the sleeping woman in his arms, his body still hard inside her. He had never expected this. Annabelle was a bundle of contradictions. When he'd thought her shy, burned by the shame of her father, now she exuded nothing but confidence. Certain she could pull off anything. She'd certainly pulled off a few tricks with him.

They'd made love. Really made love. No gimmicks, no dares. Something new and precious had connected them when she'd opened her eyes and he'd met her gaze as he'd melded his body with hers. Thoughts like this were completely foreign to him. Hell, a few years ago, the mere hint of "bonding" would cause him to cut a woman out of his life. They knew the score.

But did he? Their lovemaking surpassed sex on a desk. This was something different. Special.

He'd gag on the corny thought if it didn't ring pure and true.

Wagner loved her. His admiration and trust had

grown into love. It surprised the hell out of him, but what they shared transcended lust. What was it about her specifically, this one woman, that made him love her? Why was she different from the others?

Maybe it was because they shared a common problem. Their fathers. What was it people said about the sins of the father? Annabelle certainly wrapped herself in that cloak of shame. Arthur Scott's scams had scarred his daughter. His last swindle had been in his guise as stockbroker. He'd bilked his own relatives of their life savings and college funds.

It was that debt that Annabelle had taken upon herself, living on only the essentials, helping to repay her aunt and uncle who'd lost there life savings in her father's scheme and footing the bill for her cousin's and her own college tuition.

Annabelle made a soft noise and snuggled closer to his chest. Who'd have ever thought this would have happened? Worn out like no time ever before, his mind was fogged with the need to sleep, yet he couldn't. Surprise had lit a fire inside him. It was as if he'd finally discovered that indefinable something he had always been searching for, but never knew he wanted, was in his reach. But not quite enough. He could see that they would have to do this again. Over and over again.

9

THE POWDERY, SWEET SMELL of marshmallows tickled her nose and hauled her from the most contented sleep of her life. She slowly stretched and opened her eyes to see Wagner waving her favorite treat. A green, sugarcoated marshmallow tree.

"Mmm. Give me that." He tipped the candy toward her, running the sweet along her lips. She bit the trunk off with gusto.

Wagner leaned over and gave her a quick kiss, his tongue sweeping her lips for a taste.

"A girl could get used to this," she told him as she stacked two pillows on top of each other and slid along the silk pillowcase. "Marshmallows and kisses in the morning."

He raised an eyebrow. "Which is better?"

Like her sex maniac in bed needed any more ego stroking. Although she wouldn't mind stroking something else. Annabelle nibbled another bite. "I'll let you know," she said with a wink.

Wagner laughed, a rich deep baritone that had her toes curling into the mattress.

"I woke up hungry," he told her, reaching for a take-out foam cup from the plastic storage bin he used as a nightstand. "There's nothing to eat. The pizza fell upside down on the floor."

"Wonder when that happened?" she asked, plopping the last of the tree into her mouth. Oh, but her body remembered. It had to have been about the time he shoved everything aside and swooped her up into his arms. She could relive that moment forever and still get a giddy feeling.

"I walked down to the grocery store for some coffee, saw the marshmallows and thought of you."

"Is that good?"

He gave her another hard kiss on the mouth. "All thoughts of you are good. I also saw these." He plopped a package of gourmet cookies on the bed.

"Wow, you've been busy."

She really should mention this kind of eating in bed was developing dangerous bedtime habits, but she'd do it later. Much later. But the smell of fresh-baked cookies beckoned. Pushing away the rest of the marshmallows, she scrambled to rip the wrapping off what she swore had to be chocolate chip and peanut butter. Making hot love with Wagner, and the brief nap afterward, left her famished. Only cookies could assuage.

Then she'd start the process all over again.

The soft sheet slid down the side of her.

He rubbed a small mark on her left breast. "I didn't notice this tattoo earlier."

Heat and a slight flush infused her skin. "You were otherwise occupied at the time."

"My, my, Annabelle. You do have your little secrets. That little moon is sexy as hell."

She'd been embarrassed by the tattoo ever since she and Katie had driven down to Texas to get them. The one time her normally sleeping free spirit awoke. Now she felt only hot and excited. Wagner found her bit of daring sexy.

Wagner broke off a piece of cookie and fed it to her, his fingers tasting sweet. His groan was a painful thing ripped from his chest.

"This is hell, but I'm going to keep feeding you," he said, playful agony in his eyes.

Her thighs would pay for all these sweets later. The sit-ups wouldn't help her quads any. Annabelle paused a moment. Nope. Nothing. The thought of monstrously huge thighs just didn't seem to bother her at all.

She broke off a piece of chocolate chip cookie and fed the chewy morsel to Wagner. His lips sucked on her fingers, his tongue tasting and licking the crumbs. A thrill shuddered from her finger to her entire body.

He grabbed the remaining part of the cookie out of her hand and slid the decadent treat into her mouth. The chocolate and sugar danced on her tongue. Yummy.

"This is a good cookie for store-bought. Reminds me of my granny's."

Wagner tugged off his T-shirt, then shoved down his jeans. He slipped under the silk covers beside her, molding her body to his. Darn, he'd left on his boxers. "I've never heard you talk about her before."

"She died shortly after my dad." The strain of her son's duplicity and the scandal that followed was too much for her. Annabelle's throat tightened and she felt the familiar clog of tears in her eyes. *No.* She wouldn't let memories of her father and all his destruction ruin what she and Wagner had started just hours before. A new beginning. Maybe even a new life together.

"Granny was wonderful, Irish with a beautiful accent—a combination of her native Irish lilt and an Oklahoma twang. She told funny stories that always had a moral and I really think she believed in fairies." Annabelle closed her eyes and remembered. "But the thing I liked most about her was the nuts. I hate them."

"Uh…what? Did you say you hated nuts?" he asked, clearly confused.

"Yeah, I hate nuts."

"Nuts? How can you hate nuts?"

"I don't actually hate nuts. I mean, I'll eat them on a plane. It's just that I don't like them in fudge or brownies or in anything like that."

He plopped a hunk of cookie in his mouth. "You're kidding. That's sacrilege."

"No, nuts do not belong in any dessert, especially in chocolate chip cookies."

"I can't believe you're saying this. Nuts are what make things taste good. To think I felt bad when the store only had the plain cookies."

Now Annabelle rolled her eyes. "Granny knew I didn't like them. But the rest of the family did."

"Good taste, your family," he said dryly.

"Can I finish this story, please? Anyway, Granny knew I didn't like nuts, so whatever she was making, she would always save a little of the batter. She'd have just a little for me without any nuts."

Wagner nodded, understanding. "That's a grandma. You know, your mom would just tell you to pick the nuts out. But your grandma," he said with a smile, "she makes things special just for you."

Annabelle reached below the smooth sheet. "Of course, there are some nuts I like."

Wagner tugged her hand away. "Woman, you gotta give me at least an hour to recover."

She made a tsking noise. "Then I guess there's only one thing to do."

"What's that?"

"Watch C-SPAN."

If anyone could ever be described as springing from a bed, Wagner stood as the perfect example. "How could I have forgotten?"

"Remind me to tell you about mantras someday."

Fifteen minutes later, they were once again sitting shoulder to shoulder on Wagner's futon. But this time they sat under a blanket. Naked.

And the vote was not going well. The muscles of

his back tensed with each passing moment. The Congress members debated endlessly on the merits or problems of what Annabelle and Wagner had begun to think of as *their* bill.

At the last minute, some lawmaker had tacked on an amendment and this add-on drew ire from Congress members coast to coast.

"I can't believe this," Annabelle said as yet another Congress member stood to comment.

"An idea and my reputation. That's all I started with. Both appear to be fading fast."

"Look—" Annabelle pointed to the screen "—they're breaking for a weekend recess."

"Great. A prolonging of the agony."

Annabelle groaned. After wrapping the blanket around her body, she extended her hand. "We have forty-eight hours. It's time for a plan. First, we have to think like politicians. We identify the key leaders, we make one fall…"

"They all vote our way."

"Right. Forty-eight hours to call, e-mail and harass."

"Harass our politicians?"

"Absolutely. Who better?"

THEY LOBBIED side by side for thirty-seven straight hours. As Wagner worked the phones, she scoured the Internet learning more about each crucial member of the House. Responses from the dozens of e-mails she'd sent out earlier were beginning to fill up the in-box of her mail program. Wagner passed her desk after grabbing his third cup of coffee. She'd not fetched coffee in over a week and this morning he'd even made it.

With a rush of energy she didn't think she possessed after so little sleep, she surged to her feet, seized Wagner by the collar of his shirt and dragged him close.

The feel of his hands on her breasts made her knees go weak. "Oh, Wag," she groaned.

"You called me Wag. I like it," he said before his lips met hers again.

The telephone on her desk rang. With so much riding on a few telephone calls, Annabelle couldn't ignore the phone now. But oh, how she yearned to bask in Wagner's kiss.

With a playful bat to his hands, she picked up the handset. "Achrom Enterprises."

"How's the dry well?"

Katie. Her heartbeat skipped and panic settled along her spine. Here it was…confrontation time.

She knew something was coming. As this bill before Congress approached its day of reckoning, so did her mini-avoidance reprieve.

Okay, two options. She could play dumb with Katie or she could lie. No, no, no. The truth was always better. Only two days ago, they'd speculated Wagner's heart had stopped pumping. She eyed the man now. Shirtsleeves rolled up, tie pulled loose, hair ruffled. Oh, yeah. All warm-blooded male. The truth was much better.

"Let's just say all the equipment is in fine working order," she said, admiring the tight package of his backside. Nice. To look at and to touch.

"I knew it. I knew you were screwing the boss." Katie sounded triumphant and horrified at the same time.

She *was* screwing the boss.

Something wasn't right. Wait, everything was right. Something wasn't normal. About her. And her gut told her Katie knew what.

An odd trepidation sent her foot to tapping. Wagner turned toward her, lifting an eyebrow, but with a negative nod, she let him know the call wasn't one they'd been waiting on.

"You've been avoiding me, haven't you?" Katie went on, her voice accusatory and almost a little hurt.

Damn straight.

"No, of course I haven't been avoiding you." *Way to go, Annabelle. Can't you lie just a little more convincingly?*

"Look, we need to talk. It's important."

"Wag and I are kind of in the middle of something—"

"I need to buy some marshmallows. I need your advice, for, uh, my niece. What kind does a four-year-old like?"

Annabelle perched on the edge of her desk. "Oh, that's a very good question. Not many people know about all the various kinds of marshmallows—"

"Why don't you show me? Come on, Belle, you need to get away from the office for a bit. To shop.

Help me shop. Munch on...marshmallows. Who cares about our waists?"

"Or our thighs." When had she not cared about her thighs?

"Oh yeah...thighs. We can meet at the Bricktown Ballpark."

Ding, ding, ding. She hadn't been able to shake the urge to see the ballpark. Now. She had to see it up close. Now. And she was getting hot. Shrugging out of her lightweight sweater, she draped it across her chair.

A quick glance at the clock reminded her she had time to steal a few moments away from the office. They didn't expect anything to happen for another hour and a half. Annabelle could stay at work making out with the boss as easily as the next girl. But she needed a break. A moment to gab with her best friend about her new man. She needed to talk to Katie.

"All right. I'll meet you downtown by the fountain in ten minutes. We can walk to the ballpark together. I hope the gates are open—I'd like to see the field."

"I was afraid you might," Katie said softly.

"What?"

"Never mind. I'll explain it all when you get here."

THE FOUNTAIN WATERS jetted and danced at the mouth of the canal. With the winter chill increasing daily, fewer and fewer people sat on the benches lining the canal. In the summer, children splashed in the spray and teenagers dressed in black wove their way through the blasts of water on their skateboards. The city would be draining the canal soon. How strange it always looked, just a dry concrete bed. After the holidays, flower beds of purple and yellow pansies would be the only color. But these wooden benches, Annabelle thought, despite the temperature, always seemed to welcome her and Katie to sit, people watch and chat.

Annabelle beat Katie to their regular seat, but soon she spotted her friend carrying two foil-wrapped sandwiches. Annabelle almost did a classic comic doubletake when she noticed that conservative highlights now replaced her best friend's usual pink-tipped hair.

"What's with the change?"

Katie shook her head. "Oh, looks like I'm going to have to get a real job."

Annabelle laughed at the exaggerated disappointment in her friend's voice. "Ha. Welcome to the real world."

Katie plopped down beside her. "Speaking of the real world, which one have you been inhabiting lately?"

"What are you talking about?"

Katie nodded, a lock of her layered hair falling into her eyes. "Okay, if that's how you want to play it. But you know what? That's not gonna work. I won't let you play dumb and wiggle out of telling me the truth."

"I never play dumb."

"You know, you're right. You don't. And that's what's so scary. You're doing a lot of things you never used to do...including your boss."

"Hey, you were all for it a week ago."

"Listen to me, Annabelle. Listen to me very carefully. At that party, something strange happened to you. At first I thought Mike's attempts to hypnotize you didn't work, but now, whoa sister. I know it's all true."

Annabelle fought. Fought the haze of threatening truth. "Nothing happened to me at the party. I barely remember much about that yawner. Just a quick in and out. If things are different, attribute the changes to what we talked about before. My life is changing. I wanted Wagner in it. Since the not-so-subtle approach wasn't working, I had to take matters in my own hands. And it's great. I can't believe I waited this long. Think of all the time I wasted. I could have been having fabulous sex all along. Who denies themself like that? Who thinks of it as a challenge to see how long they can resist temptation? It's sick."

"That's emotional maturity."

Annabelle stuck out her tongue. Katie Sloan was the last person to be giving out pointers on reliability and how to behave like a grown-up. "I've given maturity up."

Katie grabbed Annabelle's hands. "Listen to me. You were hypnotized. You are going to get fired. Do you understand me?"

Nodding her head, Annabelle eyed the sandwiches in her friend's hand. "Yes. I understand."

"Whew, that's a relief."

"Don't forget, I saw the hypnosis con up close and personal. Whatever Mike did, it didn't work."

"Okay, you know what—we'll drop this for now. I'm hungry. I bought two gyros. The one without tomatoes is yours."

"I'm starting to think tomatoes might not be that bad. Being so picky may be limiting a whole wealth of foods. Maybe it's time for me to give those little red suckers a try."

Katie raised an eyebrow and shook her head. "I'm not even going to touch that. Next you'll be telling me you want nuts in your brownies." Katie handed Annabelle one of the foil-wrapped packages. "Here, knock yourself out."

Annabelle took a bite of her gyro, letting the flavors settle in her mouth. "Nope, still don't like tomatoes."

Katie handed Annabelle the other sandwich and took back the one with tomatoes.

"Hey, after we're done, let's go over to that little lingerie shop. I want something that will drive Wagner crazy."

"Hmm. How about something in fishnet?" Katie suggested, her tone odd.

Now *there* was some hosiery she could get into. "Good idea."

Katie clapped her hands. "Ah-ha. Proof. You wouldn't even be caught at a Goth party wearing black fishnet."

"I've never been to a Goth party."

"That's not the point. They're all about black and fishnet there and you'd still never wear it, even when socially appropriate."

"I, uh…"

"And tell me, you have this strange desire to see the ballpark?"

"That's no great guess—I told you I wanted to see it."

"But it's more than that, Belle. You have an urge, almost a craving you can't fight to be there."

"Look around, there's not a single blade of green grass, but if you walk a few steps and look between the slats, you see something wonderful. There's a whole field of beautiful green grass in the middle of December. Just think how wonderful it would be to run across it on bare feet, to—"

Annabelle's fingers trembled as she covered her mouth. She closed her eyes and swallowed. She glanced up at her best friend. "Did you hear what I just said? I wanted to…I wanted to run—"

"You wanted to run naked across the ballpark?"

"How did you know?"

"I was there in the room. I heard the whole thing. You really were hypnotized."

And like that…it was over.

All the little hints and the questions, they were no longer struggling to come to the surface. Now the truth burst out, no longer deniable.

The triumphant look vanished from Katie's face and her expression turned sympathetic. "I know, honey, and I'm sorry. Annabelle, you really were hypnotized. Think about how you've been acting, how you've been avoiding me."

"I, uh, I haven't been avoiding you." *Great, another failed attempt at the truth.*

Katie waved her hand. "Ask *yourself*, Annabelle. Go ahead. Ask yourself why you've been avoiding me. It's because you know."

Katie's words…they did ring true. She'd been avoiding Katie like other people avoided arranging their clothes in seasonal order. She loved organizing her closet. And she loved talking to Katie. Especially about new clothes, a new man and great sex.

And until today she'd done neither.

Her shoulders slumped.

"The hypnosis may even be wearing off already. Have you been wondering why you craved a certain thing, or suspected your behavior was a little odd? Admit it, you haven't wracked yourself with guilt over your dad in at least twenty-four hours and can't figure out why. I've been doing some research on the Internet. Put your hands together. Clasp them, like you're going to hold your own hand."

Putting her sandwich on her lap, Annabelle folded her hands. "Why am I doing this?"

"Depending which thumb is on top, that indicates whether you're more susceptible to hypnosis or not. See, your left thumb is on top."

"And that means I'm more susceptible?"

"Yes. Er, wait. Maybe it's the right thumb on top.

My right thumb is on top and I remember thinking, hmm. Why didn't I write this down? Left. Definitely the left thumb. Look, forget about the thumb. Let's face facts. You like marshmallows."

"Crave 'em."

"Been doing sit-ups?"

Annabelle patted her stomach. "Never looked better."

"How do you feel about your thighs?"

"Until this moment, I've been thigh issueless."

"And the most important part. Daring. How's the sex life? Is it more on the, uh, adventurous side?"

Desk, C-SPAN, marshmallows, Blue Boa. Heck, she could sell her stories on the Internet.

"A little more than usual," she hedged. She'd never share what they'd done with a little bit of sugar.

"And how do you feel now?"

With a sudden lurch to her stomach, the thought of another marshmallow made her sick.

Hypnotized. She'd foolishly thought she'd be immune, but the joke was on her. She'd been put under by some guy who'd learned his techniques from a book he borrowed from the library.

Annabelle itched to get her fingers onto a clip to pin up her unruly hair. She wound her fingers around a strand of hair. Down, at the office? What had she been thinking? "It's me. I'm back to the same old me."

Recalling her behavior of the last few days, her face heated with acute embarrassment. She'd done *that* to

Wagner in the supply closet. Her fingers cut into the foil of her gyro as instant regret squeezed her heart.

Katie squeezed Annabelle's shoulder. "I did the right thing. Telling you, right?"

"Yes, of course. It's like you said earlier, the hypnosis was starting to fade anyway. I was beginning to question…things. Knowing the source of my behavior will save me a bundle in not seeking therapy."

Katie glanced at her watch. "I have to go. I have a job interview at the paper in half an hour. I can cancel if you need me to stay."

"No, I'm all right."

"Really?"

Annabelle forced her lips into a big smile. "No, I'm just kind of a bummed because my stomach was looking pretty good from all those sit-ups."

Katie gave the required laugh at Annabelle's pitiful attempt at a joke. "What are you going to do?"

"Quit my job."

"Well, at least you were going to do that anyway."

Yes, but a week ago she was only lusting after the boss.

Now she loved him.

Or was that an illusion, too?

10

HIGH HEELS AND HEARTBREAK didn't mix. Annabelle dragged those heels of hers slowly back to the office. Soft and sensible would be the rule for shoes from now on. Strappy was definitely out. Strappy in the middle of December?

The rush of the city and thoughts of seducing her boss no longer buoyed her sprits but deflated them. Now the hustle of the city was reminding her she had no close family to share the upcoming holidays. She'd never again felt truly welcome in her aunt and uncle's home.

Looking through the glass office door, she spotted Wagner prowling the carpet in front of her desk. Energy fairly zapped from his skin. The late nights hadn't taken its toll on him. In fact, he appeared ready, powerful and vital.

Her shoulders slumped with a tiredness she'd never felt before.

This was the real Wagner. The commanding, potent man itching to make the deal and work the people, full of ideas and ideals, but only on his terms.

And she was back to the real Annabelle. The old Annabelle. The one he hadn't given a second glance to. Her heart ached, truly ached at the sight of him.

Would she ever rest against those broad shoulders? Turn to fire under the caress of his fingers? Hear him groan as she gave him pleasure? Revel in the even rise and fall of his chest afterward?

No.

Because Wagner didn't want or desire the real Annabelle Scott.

The merger. She'd stick by his side until this congressional vote and Wagner took his new position as COO with Anderson. Then she'd return to her old plan—credit counseling to help people be wiser with their money and not make the kind of mistakes her father had lured people into. Annabelle sucked in a breath. Katie was right. She hadn't thought about her father as much as she used to.

Wagner would probably be relieved after she left, realizing she was not the same woman who'd seduced him on his desk. But for now she'd have to act as though nothing had happened and that her heart wasn't breaking at the thought of never seeing him again.

But it was the right thing to do. For the sake of the merger. For him.

Turning the knob, she pushed open the door. When he looked up and saw her, he smiled, the tension lines running along his forehead easing. Did she do that to him?

In two long strides, Wagner reached her. Spanning her waist with his hands, he picked her up and twirled her around in his arms. With a delighted squeal, she allowed herself this one purely selfish moment of pleasure in his arms. Hadn't her heart and mind agreed to play this off cool? Now here her emotions were rebelling...

"It's working. I found the congresswoman who's holding the whole thing up. Congresswoman Taggert. I've got a call to her right now. She's from the great State of Texas. How can she not be for an ag bill?"

"That's great." Annabelle's heart bounced, then grew heavy in her chest. There would be no dragging this out, then. No last-minute savoring of being near Wagner. The bill would pass and the merger would sail through and then her time to leave loomed. Her few days might only be hours now.

Wagner nodded toward her desk. "I bought you something to celebrate."

A small box tied in a purple satin bow lay in the middle of her desk. A silver sticker with the name of a gourmet bakery indicated the box came from the high-priced shop in the lobby of their building.

With cold and shaky fingers she snaked the ribbon through the loops, savoring the smooth feel of the material on her skin, drawing the moment out as long as possible.

Wagner had bought her a present. As she lifted the lid, the scent of chocolate and sugar drew her attention. Her vocal cords constricted and several long moments crawled by before she could say anything. "You bought me cookies."

"See. No nuts."

Annabelle turned away from him, hugging the box of cookies tightly to her chest. Lovers had bought her gifts before, more expensive ones than a box of cookies. But no one had ever taken the time to pick out exactly what she liked.

Now she was going to cry.

"I just can't do it," she said, trying hard not to let him see a tear, desperately trying to hold her emotions in check.

"What do you mean, you can't do it? You can eat it later. I know you ate with Katie." His voice turned low, seductive. "We can save them for later. Maybe I'll crumble you a path to the couch to follow. You up for the X-rated version of "Hansel and Gretel"? We still haven't played out that couch suggestion you made."

Annabelle choked back a sob.

"Hey, we can make the rating R."

She jerked away when he tried to draw her near. If he touched her, she'd fold.

He reached for her, offering the comfort of his strong arms and broad shoulders. *She loved this man so much.*

He tilted up her chin. "I was just trying to make a joke. What's wrong, Annabelle? Did something happen between you and Katie?"

The concern in his voice, the tenderness of his

touch, the stirrings and promises of something more she spotted in his eyes, the fact that he gave a damn… She had to end this farce. End this sham affair now before he fell in love with something, someone she wasn't, and before she forgot she was really someone else.

She already wished, more than anything, to be the person, the Annabelle, of twenty minutes ago. And those thoughts, yearnings, could only bring her more heartbreak.

Annabelle shook her head. "I have to go."

Brainstorm. Yes, pack up and get out. Sounded like a good mantra to her. She made a dash for her desk, opening up the bottom drawer. A package of marshmallows fell onto her purse, spilling tiny green, yellow and pink globs all over her new hot 'n' handy handbag.

She slammed the drawer closed with her foot. Yanking open the middle drawer pullout, she rummaged for her keys. A bottle of polish she'd used to create "Persuasion" rolled back and forth in the pencil tray. "This isn't me. This stuff isn't mine."

Wagner placed his hands on Annabelle's shoulders and studied her face. "What are you talking about? Of course this stuff is yours."

"I mean, it's not the real me. The real Annabelle Scott. Look, I'm leaving. Don't bother sending any of this to me. I never kept anything personal in my desk anyway and this new stuff…I don't want. Just throw it all away."

"Whoa. Hold on." His grip tightened on her shoulders.

The warmth of his fingers easily seeped through the thin material of the too-sexy sundress she wore. Sundress. With open-toed shoes. To work. What in the world had she been thinking?

With a gentle tug, Wagner spun her around to face him. "You can't leave now. We're about to pull off a major legislative coup. And the best part is we're knocking Kenny Rhoads off the pedestal he put himself on."

Oh, he was gorgeous. And gazing down at her with such concern, he was everything she could ever dream of in a man. Her man. How easy it would be to loop her arms behind his neck. With little effort, she could draw his head lower, cover his lips with her own, warm herself from the heat of his skin and the passion of his soul.

Annabelle broke from his embrace and propelled herself toward the front door, her hand resting on the knob. She'd allow herself one last look. One of those long, lingering, I'll-commit-this-moment-to-memory kind of glances. A week ago, she'd sat at her desk, staring at his door, trying to convince herself to be a little daring to spark his interest. A sweater and a carpet picnic.

Her heart constricted.

Unrequited lust was a whole lot easier to deal with than a heart ground into the dirt. Pulverized by her very own, and totally impractical-for-the-office, new stiletto heel.

Now she was just glad to be herself again. Mostly. Life seemed to go a whole lot easier posthypnosis. Her problems not as insurmountable. Her seduction tactics had come naturally. Such as how she managed to pull off this totally strange paint job on her toenails... Well, that's a trick she'd like to remember.

Now she faced a truly insurmountable problem. A life without Wagner.

We. He'd said *we.*

She shook her head, clearing her mind of any *we* images his words invoked. "That's just it, Wagner. *We* didn't do anything. You made it happen. I mainly stumbled around and got lucky. Very lucky."

Wagner rounded her desk and clasped her hand, tugging her gently away from the door. "Annabelle, honestly, I don't know what's going on here. Hell, I don't know what's been going on for the last week." Wrapping his arms around her, he drew her close to his chest. "But I do know we're lucky in more ways than just this merger. We found each other, too."

Wagner didn't bother to disguise the hurt and confusion in his voice. She recognized the desperation in him because she felt it, too. Knowing the breakup had to be done, but hoping something would come along to stop it.

Annabelle blinked quickly, once again trying to contain her tears. "Oh, Wagner, this whole walk back from the fountain I tried to convince myself I could go on like I didn't know the truth. Don't you know I wish I could? But now I know I can't. It's not me. This, the heels, the sundress, this is not me."

His arms tightened around her waist. "I don't care about any of that stuff."

"It's just part of the package that finally got your attention." She sighed heavily, she shoulders slumped and her heart ached. "I'm tired. I'm tired of pretending. I just can't keep the game up anymore."

"Were you pretending about us?" A muscle flexed at his jaw, his voice flat.

Her tummy clenched. She couldn't let him think that. "No, of course I wasn't."

"I love you, Annabelle."

Well, darn. She'd wanted to hear those words all her life and here they were, out in the open for her to grab and hold dear. Blood rushed to her heart and unbelievable happiness and hope pushed new energy and excitement to every square inch of her body. A real, commit-to-memory-forever kind of moment and she had to kick it to the curb.

She twisted to look at him, the muscles of her stomach pulling tender and tight, reminding her of the hypnotic suggestion. The thought sapped her new energy, leaving her sadder than ever.

Maybe she should have let him think her desire was all make-believe. The pain would be over quickly then. Always better to be angry than brokenhearted.

"I love you, too," she said. The selfish words escaped before she could haul them back into her big mouth.

His sexy lips curved into a relieved and sexy-as-hell smile. "Then what's the problem? We're sitting on the chance of a lifetime with this merger. You love me, I love you, *this* is the way a happy ending is supposed to be. I've never said this in my whole life. Never even thought I'd want to say something like this. Let's make a happy ending."

Temptation slammed into her body. How easy and delightful it would be to lay her head down on his chest and say yes.

But how long would it be?

How long before he began to ask questions? Why was she different? What happened to her daring side?

If she left now, she could treasure that spark of love she saw glowing in the depths of his blue eyes.

No. She had to be strong and break away now. No happy ending awaited them based on something she really wasn't. One day Wagner would wake up and see the real Annabelle and be disappointed. She couldn't take the disappointment. Not from him.

"No, Wagner. You don't love me. You love someone else. Someone who wasn't really me."

"You keep saying that. What the hell are you talking about?" Frustration laced his every word.

She swallowed hard. Clean-break time. "Please believe me when I tell you that I love you, but it just isn't *me* you love. I was hypnotized. That's why I was acting so strangely. It was something the hypnosis created. I'm doing you a favor, really. You wouldn't want the real me. You didn't before."

The phone rang.

Wagner didn't move, his eyes never leaving hers.

A second ring.

Still nothing.

"Wagner, you have to get this. Your entire future rides on that call."

"Not my entire future."

Third ring.

"Answer the damn phone." Bitter desperation had her yelling. If she was going to give him up, he better damn well earn it. "Please."

Dragging his gaze away from hers, he answered, his voice sounding tired and rough. "Achrom here."

Silence stretched as he listened to the caller. Emotions played across his face. After another minute he hung up.

She walked over to him and kissed him lightly on the cheek. "Goodbye, Wagner. I'm sorry I misled you."

"It doesn't matter anyway. That was a very gleeful Kenny Rhoads. The son of a bitch managed to convince Congresswoman Taggert to table the bill. It's over. The merger's a bust."

And so was that small desperate glimmer of hope that had apparently lingered even after she told him about the hypnosis. It was all a bust.

KATIE PLOPPED the newspaper beside Annabelle as she fiddled with the computer mouse. "You should be fine-tuning your résumé or searching for employment on one of those online job-listing Web sites, rather than messing around on the Internet."

Annabelle lifted her gaze from the computer screen. "Hey, just because you finally got a respectable job doesn't mean the rest of us can't waste colossal amounts of time searching for useless information."

"I let you sulk around for two days. It's time to snap out of it."

"Hmm, maybe you can hypnotize me into someone who doesn't mope." Annabelle twined a lock of hair around her finger. Sheesh, it's a wonder she hadn't twisted herself bald. "You know, that's not a bad idea."

"Won't work now. Your subconscious is onto the game. Your mind wouldn't accept the suggestion."

"Bummer. I liked the new Annabelle much better than the old one. That Annabelle had a lot more fun. And a man. All the old Annabelle had to show was a corresponding coaster for every cup and a color-coded padded hanger for each article of clothing."

Katie fisted her hands and screamed. "Honestly, Belle, you're driving me nuts. You know who liked the old Annabelle? Me, that's who. In fact, the old Annabelle was my best friend."

"You have to say that. You're feeling guilty."

"Well, you know who else liked the old Annabelle? Wagner Achrom. In fact, he respected her enough to pay her so much money, she could pay off her father's debts and go to school. Money he could have used to keep his company afloat another few months. Maybe wait out this bill."

Annabelle resisted the urge to place her hands over her ears and block Katie's words. They were too hurtful. Too hopeful.

"But instead he's going under. And a business-man like Wagner knows the score. He knew he had the potential to lose everything when he should be cutting costs. And he still managed to find you more than your average cost-of-living increase. Prehypno-sis. I never thought I'd say this about the man, but he is actually a nice guy. Take those nut-free cookies you have zip-sealed on a place of honor on your bak-er's rack. I've dated a lot of guys and I can count using the number of noses I have how many would remember a detail like that."

With a whirl, Katie stalked to the kitchen.

"Where are you going?"

"To throw away any marshmallows you still have hiding in the cabinet."

Katie's words dragged her sagging hopes back up. Her best friend wasn't saying anything she hadn't dwelled on herself. Except before, she'd slammed those hopes right back to reality.

Okay, so getting rehypnotized was out of the ques-tion. But that didn't mean she couldn't arm herself with everything she could possibly learn about the subject. She'd avoided even the thought of hypnosis since leaving Wagner's office. Practically threw the remote into the TV screen after seeing an advertisement about losing weight with the technique.

With nervous fingers, she almost misspelled hypnotism as she typed it into the Google search engine.

Great, over seventy thousand sites appeared. She clicked on the first and began to read. How long she read, she didn't know, but Katie twisting and tying a trash sack drew her attention away from the computer.

She tapped on the screen with her finger, excitement building with each smudgy fingerprint she left on her monitor. "Read this."

"'Hypnosis cannot change a person's core personality, but rather frees the repressed self.'"

Her best friend read it again, this time more slowly.

Annabelle grabbed her hand. "Katie, do you realize what this means?" Gosh, she was almost afraid to believe what she read.

"Your behavior wasn't the hypnosis."

"Good, I wanted to make sure I was reading that right."

"You reached your potential. That's the beauty of this whole thing. You didn't have to know what you wanted, only your subconscious did. You made all this happen yourself. You made yourself get noticed, you made Mr. Monochrome fall in love with you. You and you alone. And you know what, you can get yourself out of the mess you created, too."

Annabelle shook her head in wonder. "I just still

can't believe it. It's funny. I feel relieved and betrayed at the same time."

She sat down in her favorite place in the apartment, the window seat. The window seat had sold her on the apartment. She added the soft mauve and green cushions later, but the carved seat and the large bay window was a daydreamer's paradise.

Katie joined her, fluffing a cushion on her lap. "This explains so much. Remember the tattoo?"

How could she forget? Once Wagner discovered the moon, he'd made it a point to run his tongue along each little line. Annabelle shuddered. Her body longed for his touch. She could only nod at Katie's question.

"This explains why you could get the tattoo and I couldn't."

"Pain and a needle explains why I could get the tattoo and you couldn't."

"You're getting me off the subject. You've been repressing your true self. Ever since you took on the weight of your father's debts, you've closed off the real you. The adventurous and crazy side of you. The hypnosis simply allowed parts of you to be released."

And Wagner had really liked those parts. How was he doing? She wished she could comfort him. The fuel cells he created, along with his dreams, might remain locked in his office safe.

Resting her forehead on the cold pane of glass, she closed her eyes. She felt tired, the idea of marshmallows made her sick and she could swear the sensation of her heart actually breaking made her chest ache. But if she could make a joke at her own expense…for some strange reason she felt more alive than ever.

Annabelle opened her eyes and smiled at her friend.

"You okay?" Katie asked, appearing worried.

Flashes of the Blue Boa danced in her memories. "You know what, Katie. I deserve great and daring sex."

"Now you're talking."

"I deserve to not obsess about my thighs."

"Right on."

"I deserve Wagner."

Katie wrapped her arms around her, giving her a hug. "The question is…what are you going to do about it?"

After her father's betrayal, Annabelle had never felt as if she deserved anything. But she shoved those feelings right out of her brain. Wagner was hers. Now she needed to go get him.

But how could she do that? Doubt slowly crept into her thoughts. That was a nice thing about the new Annabelle; she never had uncertainties. Or reservations.

The old Annabelle would just have to learn to ignore them.

An overwhelming sense of urgency smacked her right in the middle of her moon tattoo. She wouldn't waste time thinking of a way to get him. She'd just do it.

"I'm going to call him."

"That would be a start."

Relieved that she finally had some kind of plan, never mind that it wasn't in writing or outlined properly, she made her way to the kitchen phone and dialed his number. Actually, she had to dial his number twice, her hands were shaking so much she misdialed the first time. While waiting for him to pick up, her blood rushed so loudly she heard it in her ears.

One ring.

Maybe calling hadn't been such a good idea.

Two rings.

Maybe she should have gone to his apartment instead. Three rings.

Where was he?

Four rings.

This was all wrong. Hanging up, Annabelle raced for the computer.

"What are you doing?" Katie asked.

"This calls for something a little more daring than a phone call, don't you think?"

11

ANNABELLE GLANCED AT the crinkly sheet of paper bearing the face of the CEO of Pleasures, Inc. She'd printed the CEO's bio and pic from the company's Web site. At each stop, Annabelle studied the picture lying on the passenger side of her car for the last three hours as she drove from Oklahoma City to the Dallas-Fort Worth airport. Moments to spare. The CEO's flight would leave soon.

She had no plan.

The new Annabelle would say, "Plan splan," and go with what felt right.

The old Annabelle would say, "Oh, crap."

She'd already "spontaneously" opened Wagner's safe and borrowed a few fuel cells. Might be technically breaking and entering since she was no longer an employee, but who cared about those minute details?

Grab the CEO's attention.

Hey…where did that come from? Okay, great. That works. The beginnings of a plan. Who cared where it came from?

If she could grab the woman's attention before she

passed the security checkpoint, where no one could get past without a boarding pass, then she could wow the CEO with Wagner's solar-battery ideas.

Excellent. Spontaneous improvements to the plan were good. A nice little combination of old and new Annabelle.

Heck, she'd even buy a ticket to Hong Kong if she had to and talk nonstop to the woman during the whole half-a-day trip. She did a mental overview of her checking account. Then her savings account.

It would have to be the credit card.

But she wouldn't let a little thing like money fail her resolve. Wonderful attitude. Just the kind of notion a credit counselor should promote. But then, she'd been driving three hours with no bathroom break. Move out of her way; she was a woman on a mission. She could use the bathroom on the plane if she had to.

Darn, she shouldn't have parked in the by-the-hour lot. That would be one costly parking bill if she had to fly. Nope. She shoved that line of thinking right out of her mind. That was old, practical Annabelle thinking.

Actually, as Katie said, the old Annabelle had some good points. And so did the new one. But if she had to follow the CEO across half the globe, she would.

A small crush of people entered the lobby from the far side. She spotted her prey. The CEO of Pleasures, Inc., strode briskly, a woman of power. Rushing over to the small crowd, Annabelle pulled her hastily scribbled-at-the-red-stoplight talking-points note from her pocket. Then shoved them back in. This wasn't the time to be methodical; this was the time to be persuasive.

Unprompted and natural.

She raised her hand, blocking the woman. "Ms. Ulrich. A moment of your time."

A spark of interest touched the gray depths of the woman's eyes. An excellent start. With a small pat to her graying black hair, she flashed Annabelle a welcoming smile.

A saleswoman's smile.

Annabelle rushed to the other woman's side. "I have a few questions to ask you."

"Are you a reporter?"

"No, I'm a private citizen."

The sparkle of interest in the woman's eyes dimmed. "I'm very busy."

"Yes. Actually, yes, I am a reporter."

The older gave her a "nice try" smile. "I really don't have time for this."

"Look, ma'am, and with all due respect, I'm not going to let you get on that plane until you agree to hear me out," Annabelle said with a smile. A "re-ally-I'm-normal-not-a-stalker-just-persistent" kind of smile.

The CEO didn't look scared, just very, very annoyed. "Young lady, I'm going to alert security."

"You do that. I'll be more than happy to make a scene in this busy terminal." Annabelle dropped her purse and stood on top of the courtesy chair, hoping the people with the growing expressions of alarm were the woman's family or associates and not the kind of security personnel who spoke instructions into their wrists. Heads of multimillion-dollar companies often had security that rivaled that of elected officials. Annabelle made a big production of cupping her hands around her mouth like a megaphone.

The CEO said nothing, but didn't run for cover, either. She probably wanted to know what Annabelle had planned next. Heck, *she* wanted to know what she had planned next. Dropping her hands, Annabelle pulled out the new Blue Boa vibrator she'd bought on her way out of town.

"Put that away. Someone might think it's a weapon." The spark of interest returned to the CEO's eyes and Annabelle hopped off the chair. "That's one of our bestsellers."

"I have an idea to make it top the charts."

Ulrich tossed the heavy sweater onto a padded chair beside them.

Excitement welled inside Annabelle. *She had her.*

"Okay, I can respect a little spunk. You have three minutes."

Whew. Annabelle sat down beside her and smiled. "Ms. Ulrich, have you ever had one of these babies run out of spark at a crucial moment?"

CHASING DOWN a powerful businesswoman through the lobby of an airport and attempting to make her point to said businesswoman as she spotted, in her peripheral vision, airport security speeding toward her was easy compared to facing Wagner Achrom again.

He probably thought her one crazy lady.

Heck, she *was* one crazy lady. She loved Wagner. Only an idiot of epic proportions would push him away without giving it at least one last shot.

But she was also buoyed. Or her euphoria could be caused by a lack of sleep and near dizziness from following the broken yellow line from Oklahoma City to Dallas and back again.

She'd go with buoyed.

As she stood outside the double doors leading to Achrom Enterprises, her nerves jabbed at her resolve. Could she do it?

You made it happen.

If she still believed in mantras, that would be the one she'd use now. But it was true. Annabelle had made it happen.

Made Wagner want her.

Made Wagner love her.

Made the CEO of Pleasures, Inc., listen to her.

And it would be Annabelle, the old, new, real, hypnotized or whatever who would make something happen now. Her body nearly vibrated with her need to confront Wagner.

She twisted the knob. Locked. Luckily, she'd not followed her earlier impulse to leave her keys on Wagner's desk after grabbing the fuel-cell prototype. Probably still breaking and entering, but she'd already done it once—couldn't leave that single attempt alone at the party.

Turning the key, she shoved the door open, ready to start. She found Wagner carefully packing the contents of her desk into a large cardboard box, his face an agonizing blend of sadness and anger.

And her heart did a double take. In jeans and a T-shirt, Wagner looked about as devastating as he did in his monochrome power suit.

But not naked.

Naked, Wagner took devastation to whole new levels.

He turned and looked at her; his gaze was cold and angry. She swallowed. The look in his eyes would send even a Harley-riding biker dude running.

"That door was locked."

"Hi." Great, inane. Always a good, impressive start.

He returned his attention to the box. "You can take this with you."

You made it happen.

Okay, she was not going to let him turn his back on her. Not after near humiliation and arrest. After closing the distance between them, she grabbed him by the cotton of his oxford shirt and spun him around.

"Give me a phone call. That's all I ask. Then I'll leave and never darken your doorstep again. There's someone in Hong Kong who wants to talk to you."

Annabelle released the tight hold she had on the

material of his shirt with his curt nod. She leaned on her desk and dialed the country code and number for Cynthia Ulrich's hotel room. Then she depressed the speakerphone.

"Mr. Achrom, I didn't believe Annabelle at first when she said this little battery thing would virtually never run out, but I have had the Blue Boa on since I put it in my carry-on luggage in Dallas and it's still going. If anything, it seems to be getting, um, stronger."

Wagner turned a sharp glance in her direction. "I, uh, loaned Ms. Ulrich one of the fuel-cell prototypes."

"Who does she work for?"

"She the CEO of Ple—"

"Mr. Achrom, I tell you, this vibrator won't quit."

"Vibrator?"

"The Blue Boa. You should have seen the look on the man's face at customs. Things you gotta do for work, right?"

"Right." Wagner still wore that delicious look of confusion.

"Mr. Achrom, I want the exclusive rights to this fuel cell."

"Oh?" All confusion vanished. Business Wagner in action. Annabelle slipped out of the office as he reached for a notepad and red pen.

THE KNOCK AT HER DOOR several hours later wasn't unexpected. It was about time, in fact. The overcoat she was wearing was a little too hot in her apartment.

After cinching the belt, she opened the door. What she hadn't anticipated was Wagner's harsh expression. She'd expected him to be joyful, relieved at the news he no longer needed a member of Congress or the Anderson people for solvency.

Annabelle stood before him, silent. She had no tricks. No crotchless panties, no daring moves. She was just…herself as she invited him in.

Wagner stalked to the middle of the living room and turned to face her. Something electric yet subtle lurked in the depths of his blue eyes. Something wasn't right.

"Did Ulrich not offer you a deal?"

His shoulders relaxed and the lines running along his strong forehead lessened. "Yes, and it's better than I'd ever imagined. I've even secured front money. Before I came over, I called Smith and Dean to tell them to, uh…" His words trailed.

"Go take a hike?" she offered.

Wagner nodded. "Yes, that's exactly what I told them." His tone chilled, ruthless.

She shivered. Before her stood the Wagner she'd heard about. The merciless hunter. "So, you're back in business?"

"Better than ever before. I came to say thank-you."

"You're welcome."

His lips softened for a moment. Then whatever elusive spark she saw in his eyes hardened. "Goodbye, Annabelle."

His words, his tone, his attitude all said this was final.

He radiated unattainable.

With one last look, Wagner pivoted and strode to the door.

And she almost let him.

"Wait. Is that it? All I get?"

Wary eyes met hers.

"Listen to me, I waved a vibrator in the middle of the Dallas/Fort Worth airport for you. There are a few things you need to hear. Things are clear for me now."

"Doesn't matter."

"It does. I was confused before. I know this sounds unbelievable, but I really was hypnotized. I thought when we made love and when you said you loved me, well, I thought it wasn't really me. That you said and did those things with someone who wasn't me, and I couldn't take that, because…"

A tight ache pulled at the back of her throat. "I couldn't take that because I've loved you for so very, very long."

A brief flicker of hope flashed in his eyes, then died. His expression didn't change. Cold and without emotion.

"But now I understand it *was* me all along."

His eyes turned the color of ice. "Still doesn't matter."

Annabelle grabbed his shirt again. "Stop saying that. It does matter. I love you. You love me. We *can* be together. Nothing is stopping us."

His expression could have been carved from stone, hard and flinty. "I'm stopping it." The words were ground out from somewhere dark and pain filled.

She clutched his shirt tightly between her fists, squeezing the material between her fingers.

"When you walked out a few days ago, you did us both a favor. This thing between you and me, it would be my mother and father repeating itself all over again. Sooner or later, I'd see the love you have for me run cold. Your dreams crushed. I've done some pretty low things in my business life and I'm not going to start all over again dragging you down with me, like a selfish bastard, just because I want you."

Her ire rose. Something she could attribute to dear old Granny. She was more than just nut-free cookies. And Annabelle was more than something he could be valiant about. "Ah, now everything is making sense. I see what's going on. I'm not the one you want to redeem…it's you. You can't push me away to prove how noble you are. Pushing me away doesn't make you selfless. It makes you stupid. You're not your father. I'm not your mother. This isn't history repeating itself."

"That cloud of shame about your father follows you wherever you go."

His bitter words hung at her heart. She had to break through; she had just this one chance. If she blew it here, they'd both lose.

"You're right."

Wagner lifted an eyebrow. "Katie's been telling me for years that I wear his guilt and misdeeds around my neck like most women wear a teardrop necklace. I finally realized how true that was as I drove the four hours to Dallas, turning around and driving four hours right back. I didn't steal and lie. My father did. I did the best that I could to repair the damage and now I'm moving on. I'd like you to be by my side."

"It won't work. I know what can happen—I saw it with my mom."

His wounds ran deep, eroding his ability to allow a woman closer than surface level. "Wagner, we're different people. Different from your parents. First of all, I'm not about to let you shut me out. Second, and get this straight, I'm saying it loud and clear, we'll be a team. I'll be at your side and you'll be at mine."

The muscles running along his jaw tightened. Annabelle reached and stroked his stubbled cheek. "I'm not your mother. My dreams don't depend on my man…on you. My dreams are my own, but I want to share them with you. I plan to have my own career, too. I spent the longest four years of my life to get a paper telling me I can practice that career."

He grabbed her hands, pulling them from his body. But grasped her fingers tight. "What if it fails and we lose everything?"

"Then we lose everything and start all over again. Together. Side by side. Look at it this way, with my job, I can be your sugar mama."

Despite the brief flicker of hope she saw fire up in his eyes, he shook his head.

Shaking her hair about her shoulders, Annabelle gripped the ties of the overcoat. Wagner was all about concrete example. Not abstracts. Time to show him something solid.

"I don't have anything." Unlooping the coat ties, she let the material fall slowly down her back. The fabric bunched at her hips, revealing her nakedness.

Wagner sucked in a breath as her nipples grew darker and hard. His gaze traveled up and down her body, resting briefly on her breasts then slid back to her eyes.

"You've got everything," he said. His voice rasped husky and thick, raw with need.

"No, I mean I have no gimmick, no shtick. Only me." Heart pounding, she loosened her hold on the coat, the satin lining brushing smoothly past her thighs and down her calves to slide silently to the carpet.

"What are you doing to me?"

"Proving how stupid turning us down would be."

"Annabelle, I'm trying to do the right thing here. I love you too much to drag you down with me."

"Who is dragging? Thanks to the both of us, you're now sitting on a huge deal that will keep us in marshmallows and nut-free cookies for the rest of our lives. But the key in the deal…us. We're a great team. In and out of bed."

At the word *bed*, Wagner groaned, deep and full

of wanting and pain. With a tug to her hand, Annabelle was in his arms. He held her there, running his palms up and down her back. She knew the pain he was letting go of and the uncertainty he was now embracing. He'd used his parents as a crutch for too long, but sometimes crutches were a comfort. And he'd just kicked his to the curb.

"I'm putting some of the money we get from Plèasures into an annuity in *your* name. You'll never be left broke by me."

She nodded into the softness of his T-shirt. She'd won. They both had.

"It may be a rough ride. Deals fall apart."

"If they do, I have a little airport technique I can try on a certain member of Congress."

Wagner stiffened.

"Are you disappointed that things didn't work out the way you wanted?"

"No. Although, I thought I'd be doing the world a favor by creating cheap, clean power."

"Hey, don't knock the Blue Boa and its kind. You're still doing the world a favor."

"You do have a point. And I may take you up on your offer to meet with Taggert. This airport technique sure convinced Ulrich. What exactly did you do?"

Annabelle raised on tiptoe and kissed the bare skin of his neck. "I'll tell you about it tomorrow."

"Ah, but tomorrow I have big plans for you. You get to call Kenny Rhoads and—"

"Tell him to jump in a lake?" Annabelle laughed.

"Actually, I heard on the radio driving into town he was arrested for several counts of fraud and money laundering. None of his backers will touch him and his family hasn't even bailed him out of jail."

A smile played on Wagner's lips, then just as quickly as it appeared it vanished. His hands dropped from her sides and he took a step back. "I love you, Annabelle. More than I ever thought possible. But I'll give you one chance to change your mind. A get-out-of-deal-free card. If we make love tonight, I won't let you go."

"That's very generous of you."

"I'm confident. You can't seem to get enough of my body."

"What if I say no?" she asked. She'd learned it was never a good thing to keep a man too confident.

"You won't."

"Yeah, I won't."

Before his lips crushed to hers, he whispered, "I didn't think so."